MAIN STREET
Goodbye, Desert Rose

Other **MAIN STREET** *Books by*
Susan E. Kirby
from Avon Camelot

MAIN STREET: LEMONADE DAYS
MAIN STREET: HOME FOR CHRISTMAS
MAIN STREET: HOME FRONT HERO

Author SUSAN E. KIRBY's memories of Route 66, which travels past her childhood home at Funks Grove, Illinois, and on southward to her present home in McLean, include the evolution of the highway from two lanes to four. Upgradings and entire new alignments enabling faster, safer travel reflect the progressive spirit of America's Main Street. The economic survival of Route 66 communities suddenly bypassed in the process inspired GOODBYE, DESERT ROSE, a tribute to one such hardy Arizona town.

MAIN STREET
Goodbye, Desert Rose

SUSAN E. KIRBY

AN AVON  CAMELOT BOOK

MAIN STREET: GOODBYE, DESERT ROSE is an original publication of Avon Books. This work has never before appeared in book form. Any similarity to actual persons or events is purely coincidental.

AVON BOOKS
A division of
The Hearst Corporation
1350 Avenue of the Americas
New York, New York 10019

First Avon Camelot Printing: February 1995

CAMELOT TRADEMARK REG. U.S. PAT. OFF. AND IN OTHER COUNTRIES, MARCA REGISTRADA, HECHO EN U.S.A.

Printed in the U.S.A.

OPM   10 9 8 7 6 5 4 3 2 1

For Fayetta Mitchell,
friend to all of God's critters

ACKNOWLEDGMENTS

The author expresses her gratitude to Ed Edwards at the Mohave County Historical Society in Kingman, Arizona, for generously answering questions regarding Route 66, gold mining, and sundry things concerning Oatman's colorful history; to Helen Graves for her memories of Oatman, Arizona, as it was in her childhood; and to Kelly Grissom, the wild horse and burro specialist with the Bureau of Land Management in Phoenix, for sharing his impressive knowledge of wild burros.

Creative license was taken in naming the town's businesses; and the characters, of course, are all fictional.

One

Oatman, Arizona
September 17, 1952

The air-cooling system in Cactus Jack's couldn't keep up with the heat of the kitchen. It seemed to ten-year-old Kathleen Fanta as if she'd been washing dishes since her feet hit the floor that morning. She whisked dark bangs from her brow and called, "Can I go now, Mama?"

"Yes you may, darlin', you've been a big help. See if you can find Daddy. The lunch crowd's thinned out, but Cookie's leaving early, so I'll be needing some help." Mama closed the door to the pie case and emptied her hands long enough to tally a grease-splotched ticket.

"Where is Daddy?"

"He went to Solomon Sal's. Something about an old lantern."

Kathleen uncoiled a couple of yards of apron strings and gave the soppy thing a pitch.

Mama spared her a measuring glance. "You're looking washed out. Did I give you your medicine this morning?"

Kathleen crossed her fingers behind her back. "Seems like you did."

"Why don't you stretch out and rest when you get back?"

Kathleen wrinkled her freckled nose. There'd been a holiday from school due to an important town meeting. She had no intention of being so wasteful with what remained of the afternoon.

Seeing as much, Mama coaxed, "Do you good, Kathleen."

"But I'm not tired."

Too busy to argue, Mama tunneled her pencil into straw-colored hair and put what was left of the pie away. She called out, "Hold the hot peppers on that last order, Cookie."

Wesley Wright was the cook's name, but the Fantas had fallen into the habit of calling him Cookie. The stains and splatters on his apron had more to say about the past few hours than he ever would. Cookie just wasn't a talker.

"How come you're taking off early?" Kathleen tried to wring a few words from him.

"Business."

"What kind of business?"

"Personal." His muscles flexed as he flattened a burger to the grill. Dancing grease sizzled and hissed.

"Something to do with the town meeting?"

Cookie declined to say.

"You can tell me," she coaxed. "I'm good at keeping secrets. Especially the personal kind."

"Rose Kathleen!" said Mama sharply. "Post the supper special in the front window on your way out."

Kathleen taped the paper to the wide window, then

stepped outside to be certain it was centered. Cactus Jack's used to be a saloon. The name was lettered in gold leaf on the plate glass window. Years ago when Daddy and Mama had gone into the restaurant business, Daddy'd wanted to preserve the elegance of that window. So they kept the name and worked hard at wooing customers off Highway 66.

Kathleen's fingers curled into her palms as she gazed down the dusty pavement that doubled as Oatman's Main Street. Traffic traversed the twisting mountainous road and crawled right past their front door. But for how long? And what would they do when it stopped?

It'd been an ongoing concern for the town since building the new stretch of 66 was approved more than three years ago. The United States government had said the twisty road was "a risk to national security" where military traffic was concerned. Now, with the new high-speed, grade-free road about to open, Oatman's security was at risk! The local coffee drinkers, coffee cuppers, as Mama called them, talked of little else these days. Solomon Sal said, "God'll provide," and Mama, a firm believer in prayer, chimed agreement. But Daddy's fear of the worst showed in a face that twitched and hands that were never still.

Kathleen's family used the back as well as the up-stairs rooms of Cactus Jack's as living quarters. A door near the storeroom opened into a small hallway with their parlor just beyond. Kathleen scuffed through in her boots and climbed the creaky wooden stairs to change her damp and clinging shirt. Grabbing her cowboy hat and a floppy straw one for her burro, Biscuit, she raced down again and out the door.

The backyard was fenced in to protect Mama's chick-

3

ens from predators. It was sturdy enough fencing to keep Biscuit from straying as well. Daddy had wood-burned a sign reading HOME-GROWN CHICKENS 'N' BISCUIT and tacked it to the gate. But that was before this high-way business had taken a toll on his sense of humor.

Kathleen spotted her burro crowding the fence sur-rounding Mama's peach tree. Intended to keep Biscuit from destroying the tree, the encircling wire swallowed up most of the shade.

"This'll cool you down," Kathleen fanned the little burro with the straw hat. He was a deep brown color, except for his tummy. It was round and full and stood out creamy white against all that darkness. Kind of like Elephant Tooth Rock, standing pale against the dusky desert mountains that embraced the town. The similarity ended there, for the majestic quartz rock was the town's most prominent landmark and Biscuit was just one of many desert burros. Sweet as a kitten, though. He sub-mitted to the hat without a fuss. Kathleen stroked his nose. "That's my sweet Biscuit. I love you."

The little burro was named for the biscuit he'd stolen from Kathleen's high chair tray when she was just a baby. Now he stretched his neck and showed his teeth. Kathleen flashed a cheesy smile back and attached reins to his homemade string halter. She opened the gate. They headed out past Lee's Lumber Company and on to Solomon Sal's Thrift shop at the edge of town. She passed Fawn Leroy and her mama coming out of the Post Office. Fawn fell back a few steps where her mama couldn't see and poked out her tongue at Kathleen. Kathleen retaliated in kind and kept right on going.

Solomon Sal's paint-bare building of clapboard and corrugated tin was crowded with all sorts of secondhand

4

stuff. A crude bench and a soda pop machine hugged a sloping porch. Mining relics cluttered the sun-baked earth, elbowing yuccas and cactuses and a lone palo-verde for space.

Kathleen rode Biscuit around back to the old wooden water trough Miss Solomon kept filled for the wild burros. The burros were descendants of those that had once been used in the mines. Mining here once thrived but eventually declined until the mines were shut down altogether during World War II. The burros, however, had not declined. They roamed free in the desert and browsed at the outskirts of town, eating bushes and flowers and anything green. They were particularly partial to garbage. A lot of folks thought them a nuisance. But not Solomon Sal. She had a heart for all God's critters.

Miss Solomon's lingerie was pegged to the clothesline. Kathleen tied Biscuit to the rickety post with a rope left just for that purpose. "Sip your water and leave Miss Solomon's wash alone, you hear?"

Biscuit swished his tail and dipped his head toward the water trough. Satisfied, Kathleen started toward the back door of Miss Solomon's shop. But a few feet short of it, she stopped. Her nose twitched. *What was that peculiar odor?* Smelled like burning weeds. She swung around and blinked in alarm. There was a thin puff of smoke drifting out a knothole in Solomon Sal's toolshed!

TWO

Kathleen leaped around a barrel cactus and jerked open the door. Her best pal Binky Doolittle sprang up off an old crate, all puffy cheeked. His guilty face sagged relief when he saw it was only her.

Kathleen reeled back and pinched her nose. "*Phew!* Where'd you get that stinky thing?"

"In front of the theater." Binky wagged the cigar butt between his thumb and finger.

Richie Smith popped out from beneath a broken-down paymaster's table, a cigar stub clutched between his teeth. "Captain Slade lost it between the cracks in the planks. You want a puff?"

Kathleen wagged her head, stomach reeling just at the smell. Richie clucked like a chicken. She ignored the insult. There were other things on her mind. Daddy didn't like crowds and Mama'd been unable to get away for the town meeting, and Kathleen was impatient to find out what had happened.

"Is the meeting over?"

Both boys nodded yes.

"What'd they say about the Jubilee?"

"Myrt Myers said a celebration was a dumb idea when that new road's going to be the ruination of us all," said Binky.

"But Captain Slade argued that if we go out, we should go out with a bang, not a whimper," Richie chimed in.

A local war hero of diminishing reputation thanks to his gambling escapades, Captain Batch Slade had suggested the Jubilee at a previous town meeting aimed at keeping Oatman from becoming a ghost town once the new highway opened. But the townspeople, suspicious of self-serving motives, couldn't make up their minds whether or not to go along with the idea.

"So what'd they decide?" prompted Kathleen.

"They voted it in," Richie beat Binky to the punch. "Jack-drilling and pie-eating and coaster races down the hill and all sorts of big plans. A shebang to top anything ever seen in this town, the Fourth of July doings included."

"What about the kids' burro race?"

"That passed too."

Kathleen yipped for joy. "Did they set a date?"

"October eighteenth," said Richie.

"That's only a month away! Binky! We'd better start practicing."

"I'm not entering."

Kathleen's jaw dropped. "Binky Doolittle, you've got to be kidding!"

"What's the point? They're saying Captain Slade bought the burro that won the Black Mountain race," said Binky.

That race started in the foothills and progressed

through and across the Black Mountains. The tough, rugged race had been the captain's inspiration for a shorter version for children. Alarmed, Kathleen asked, "Who's he getting to ride it?"

"His niece, Fawn Leroy. That's what Myrt Myers said, anyway. And you know she's nearly always on the money when it comes to stuff about Captain Slade." Richie whistled his "s" sounds, mocking old blue-haired Myrt, who supplied his mother's beauty shop with all the latest gossip.

"Fawn Leroy doesn't even like burros," objected Kathleen. "Ever since she moved here last year, she's complained they're pesky and noisy and dirty."

"She'll change her mind, once she sets eyes on that winning burro."

"She sure rubbed our nose in it when she won the school spelling bee," Binky muttered glumly.

"And Chorus Member of the Month," said Richie.

"And Most Improved Math Student."

"And Gold Star Author."

Kathleen winced at the reminder. She still thought *her* story about Biscuit was better than Fawn's tale about the little cactus mouse whose mother wouldn't let her out of the nest for fear of owls and snakes and hungry coyotes. "She wore that dumb paper star until it fell apart," Kathleen grumbled.

"Because she loves winning," said Binky. "That's why I know she'll race."

"What about her mother?" challenged Kathleen, for Mrs. Leroy, the Captain's sister, was awfully fussy about Fawn. A crack seamstress, she decked Fawn out in prissy dresses and kept her fair curls shining. Fawn looked more like a paper doll cut from the pages of a

8

magazine than a real live girl. "Why, she wouldn't even let Fawn go on the class trip to Grand Canyon for fear she'd fall over the edge."

"I'm betting she won't want to disappoint the Captain, him being a war hero and all. They say he's still got bullets in him," said Binky.

Kathleen snorted disbelief.

But Richie nodded knowingly. "Too close to his innards to operate. Why, he could croak anytime and leave his money and his mining stock to his sister and Fawn."

"Doesn't even *like* burros. But she's going to ruin it for those of us who do," muttered Binky.

"I know! Let's send Fawn a note, warning her not to race or she'll be sorry." Richie's eyebrows shot so high, they looked like wiper blades on his forehead. "Then we'll sneak spiders into her bed just to show her we mean business."

"A tarantula. That'll fix her!" said Binky.

Tarantulas in these parts were harmless, though you'd never convince Fawn Leroy. One had crawled over her foot once at school. She'd become so hysterical, the teacher couldn't do a thing with her. But as much as Kathleen enjoyed a good prank, she was pretty sure they wouldn't get past Fawn's mama. One other thing Gwen Leroy was fussy about, and that was Fawn's playmates. She started to say so. But something in Binky's face distracted her.

"You're green!"

Misunderstanding, Binky defended hotly, "Jealous? Of Little Lady Fawn Leroy? Not me!"

"No, Binky. You really *are* green. Green as the bark on a paloverde. You better get some air." Kathleen stopped short as the shed door opened. There stood Solomon Sal in her felt hat, faded shirt, and patched jeans tucked into run-down boots.

Richie's smouldering stub disappeared behind his back, but Binky got all flustered and shoved his cigar hand in his pocket.

Solomon Sal coughed and fanned the air and studied them as if time had no end. Unnerved by the silence, Kathleen blurted, "Mama sent me for Daddy. I better get him and be on my way."

Solomon Sal tipped back her hat and scratched a squiggly blue-veined patch of forehead that the sun never touched. "Your mama can wait long enough for you youngsters to explain all this smoke."

"We . . . ah . . . that is . . ." It was as if a log got jammed in that space between Binky's front teeth. The words just stopped. Sweat beaded his brow. He moaned and clutched his belly.

Earnest as a Sunday-morning preacher, Richie took up the telling. "We saw smoke coming from your shed, Miz Solomon. Naturally, we looked to see the cause of it. And what do you think, but somebody'd left this old cigar burning."

The pleats in Solomon Sal's ancient brow deepened. The truth was bubbling up in Kathleen, just begging to be told. But she was no tattler. No, sir, she was not. Beside her, Binky plucked at his jeans and made a gurgling noise. A prelude, she was sure, to a stomach about to pitch. She edged out of harm's way.

"Truth is Miss Solomon, Captain Slade dropped a cigar in front of the theater," Binky began, his ears flushed. "Richie 'n me found it and hid out here in your shed to . . . E-e-i-i-p-e-s!"

"Your pants!" squealed Kathleen.

"You're on fire!" Richie lunged and knocked Binky to the ground. But in his haste to put out the fire, he rolled Binky within kissing distance of a pencil cactus. Binky yowled like the loser in a cat fight. He staggered up beating at his trousers and dived for the water trough. Biscuit leaped back with a startled bray and snapped the clothesline post in two. The rope recoiled like a spring. The clothespins and Solomon Sal's undergarments skimmed across the surface of the water. Binky bobbed up, a brassiere strap encircling his neck. He plowed water, sputtering, struggling, trying to climb out of the trough. But the brassiere and the weight of the garments stringing after choked him back.

"Help!" he gurgled.

"Hold still, child!" Solomon Sal set about untangling the unlikely noose. "There now. You're free."

"Th-th-thanks," stammered Binky, pale and bug-eyed.

"I dare say . . ." Miss Solomon's wrinkled-up mouth wiggled. "That is to say . . . Oh dear." Eyes bright as a cactus wren, Oatman's pearl of wisdom clutched her sides and squeezed herself so tight, a whole spasm of giggles exploded from her dusty old lungs.

Kathleen could feel Binky's pride throbbing like a mangled thumb. He was sick as a tarred dog and half-strangled by Miss Solomon's unmentionables. And in front of Richie, too. She tried to be a true-blue friend, bunching up her lips tight against her teeth and lowering her gaze to her scuffed boots.

"I'm sorry, child. Truly, I am. But what a picture!" Solomon Sal slapped her thigh and hollered and laughed.

All that merriment was a feather tickling Kathleen's

belly. The snickers mounted like tinder. Richie's titters did her in. Once sparked, she couldn't hold back any longer.

" 'The prudent see danger and take refuge,' " quoted Miss Solomon when she finally regained control. She swiped at the tears rolling down her seamed cheeks. " 'But the simple keep going and suffer for it.' "

Binky pulled at his trousers and muttered threats at both Kathleen and Richie. Solomon Sal took pity and flung an arm over his shoulder. She drew him toward the shop.

"There, there. May as well learn. 'Laugh and the world laughs with you. Cry and you cry alone.' Come along and we'll doctor. I've got some pretty good animal salve from the veterinarian down in Kingman. Takes the sting right out of a burn. Got some tweezers, just made for pulling cactus spines. Ointment, too, to ward off infection. And how about a dose of warm soda water to settle that upset stomach?"

Richie trailed along after the pair. But Biscuit was ambling off, dragging the snapped clothesline post behind him. Kathleen let out a shrill whistle and raced to catch up. She untangled him from the post and led him around front. She was looping the rope to the hitching post when she spotted her father out at the edge of the highway. His hands were in motion, from pocket to brow to rubbing his chin.

"Daddy?"

A face-muscle twitched.

She tugged at his hand. "What're you doing?"

"Listen!"

Kathleen turned her head just like his, but heard nothing. "To what?"

"The silence. Don't you hear it?"

Kathleen looked down Oatman's Main Street, then back through the Black Mountains toward Sitgreaves Pass. There wasn't a car in sight. Her father's hand trembled. "What's happened?"

"The traffic's stopped," he said in a flinty voice. "It's the new road, Kathleen. They've opened the new road."

Three

Captain Batch Slade rattled down from Sitgreaves Pass and into town in his big Buick convertible. He waved his fedora and showed off his new front teeth, hollering, "They've cut the ribbon. The traffic's all been routed south of the mountains."

So this was it, then. The moment the whole town had dreaded. Kathleen's gaze moved from the empty road to Daddy and back again. The bleakness in his face made her belly clench. She'd run home and tell Mama. See if she had any new thoughts. Or if she was still counting on God. On her way to the hitching rail, Kathleen remembered Mama's message. She relayed it and asked, "Are you coming?"

Daddy waved her on, saying, "I'll be along shortly."

Kathleen climbed aboard Biscuit and started back toward Cactus Jack's. She stopped at the post office and dialed the box open. There was a letter from Gram Sophie and Grandpa Dave, who were coming to visit next month, plus a statement from the doctor who prescribed that awful-tasting medicine Mama spooned down her

14

each morning. The third letter had to be from Mama's brother Razz. He was the only one who addressed his letters using Mama's childhood nickname, Suker, instead of Susan. Looked all right in writing. But it was odd-sounding.

Favoring the shade of store awnings, Kathleen disregarded public opinion concerning burros on sidewalks and continued along the planks, saying it over and over. "Suker, Suker, Suker." Saying it out loud to fill her head so she didn't have to think of Daddy's hand trembling.

Old Coot was lounging on the portico of the Oatman Hotel. He'd swapped his desert hat for a Giants baseball cap and was listening to a ballgame on the radio. There was room to spare, but he straightened against the adobe wall, folded up his outstretched legs, and bleated, "Get that dad-blamed burro off the walk!"

Old Coot had been sore at the world ever since he'd lost his pickup truck to Captain Slade in a card game, then popped the Captain's front teeth loose in a fit of poor sportsmanship. Now the arthritic old prospector was stuck with a big dentist bill. Plus, he had to hobble on foot each day from his sheepherder's wagon on the outskirts of town to his customary lounging spot in front of the hotel. Overlooking the old fellow's grumpiness, Kathleen guided Biscuit through portico arches and onto the street's shoulder and called back, "They've opened the new road, Mr. Coot."

"Confounded government nonsense!" Old Coot gave it momentary attention, then returned to his ballgame. "Come on, Willie. Come on! Hit that dad-blasted ball!"

The news was spreading through town quicker'n a match to a fuse. Most people were taking a sharper

15

interest than Old Coot. Folks filed out of shops and gas stations and places of business in the heat of the day. Eyes shaded. Fanning hot shiny faces. Looking so intent, as if by sheer mind power, they could suck some traffic down Main Street.

Cookie's pickup truck came up the street, bluegrass whining over the radio. He'd changed his shirt and his hair was slicked back. He pitched out the matchstick he'd been chewing and rattled on past, seeming not to notice he had the road all to himself.

Kathleen turned Biscuit into the chicken yard, then let herself in through the kitchen. Mama was alone in the restaurant, sitting down for a change, sipping iced tea. Dried perspiration stains shadowed her white waitress dress and her lipstick was just a pale memory.

"Find him?"

"Daddy's at Miss Solomon's, like you said. He'll be along shortly." Kathleen dug at the waistband of her pedal pushers and sent Mama a seeking glance. "Guess you heard about the road?"

Mama nodded.

"What're we going to do?"

"What's there *to* do?"

Kathleen flattened her mouth.

Mama sighed and tried to cheer her, saying in jest, "Tell you what—let's just close this joint and go on holiday. Anyone for tea and crumpets with the queen?"

Her imitation of Uncle Razz's English war bride reminded Kathleen of the letters in her pocket. She passed over the mail and started away, saying, "If Binky should come, send him back to the parlor. We've got things to discuss."

16

"Oh?" Mama paused, Gram's letter in hand, and shot her a look that invited further explanation.

"Burro business. They voted to go along with Captain Slade's Jubilee."

"Nothing that brings business to town can hurt." Mama followed her through the restaurant kitchen.

"They're going to have the burro race, too."

Mama smiled and said, "Good luck, then."

"Looks like I'll be needing it, cause from what I hear, Captain Slade's bringing in an out-of-town burro." Frowning, Kathleen continued, "Do you think that's fair, Mama?"

"Captain Slade is a little old for burro racing," Mama ran her finger beneath the envelope flap, making a jagged tear.

Kathleen explained about Fawn Leroy.

"Mrs. Leroy, letting Fawn have a burro? I don't think even Captain Slade can swing that one," said Mama. She withdrew Gram's letter from the envelope.

"But if it *is* true, is it fair?"

"Fair play has never been Captain Slade's long suit. That's partly what gets folks so riled at him. But then again, who says the swiftest burro will cross the finish line first?"

Mama made a good point. Burros were even less predictable than people. Some were skittish and cautious, some gluttons, some stubborn, some curious, some as crotchety as Old Coot. A teachable personality such as Biscuit's could go a long way toward winning the race.

The parlor was a boxy room with tall windows and heavy drapes. Years of desert sun had faded the rug that covered most of the floor. There was a lumpy velvet sofa against one wall. The sofa wheezed dust when you

17

sat down. Daddy figured the couch had come from the east when the century was new and Oatman was a booming gold mining town. Ordinarily, Mama didn't share his infatuation with old relics, preferring modern things. But even she thought the fabric and the intricately carved arms of the sofa were "rich-looking".

Kathleen stretched out in front of the floor fan. She rested her chin on her hands. There was nothing cool about the air coming through. But she liked to feel it wafting over her face and sifting through her hair. She closed her eyes, inched closer to the protective plastic grid, and hummed a monotone. The vibration of the fan added a rumbly tremor. By and by, she hummed herself to sleep.

"Whatcha doing?"

Kathleen bolted awake. She rolled over on one elbow and blinked up at Binky. "Nothing. Where's Richie?"

Binky shrugged. "He got tired of waiting on Solomon Sal's doctoring, I guess."

Kathleen stretched refreshed limbs. "Feeling better?"

Binky nodded and dropped down on the floor. He crowded against her, horning in on the fan. Glad for the company, Kathleen let him have the good side and crawled around to the back of the fan.

"Were you burned bad?"

"Crisp as toast," said Binky.

"Bet it leaves a scar."

Binky snickered at the way the whipping blade quivered her words. "A Frankenstein scar."

"A ghostly Frankenstein *cigar* scar. Oooh-ohhh!" Kathleen called back.

"A ghostly, black as tar, Frankenstein cigar scar. Oooh-ooh!" Binky kept up the haunt.

The rhymes got so bad, they caught the giggles. Kathleen crawled back around to the front of the fan and introduced a more serious note.

"I've been thinking—why don't we sneak up to Fawn's house and see if she's got a burro?"

"Sneak?" echoed Binky.

"We don't want her to know we're worried about it, do we?" reasoned Kathleen.

"I guess not."

Kathleen pushed her feet into her secondhand cowboy boots. Solomon Sal had sold them to her real cheap, saying they hadn't much wear left in them. But they were red. Kathleen loved anything red. She grabbed her hat and trailed after Binky.

"Where are you two headed?" Mama asked as Kathleen and Binky shot through the back kitchen.

"No place special," Kathleen made her voice casual.

"I'm working on a carryout order for Mr. Wilson. Would you drop it off at the barber shop, please?" It was more of an order than a question. Mama gave Kathleen and Binky each a bottle of Delaware Punch soda, and said that Gram Sophie and Grandpa Dave would arrive for their visit on Columbus Day, if all went as planned.

"Will they be here for Jubilee?" asked Kathleen.

"Should be," said Mama. "They're staying a week."

"Goody! They can watch Biscuit and me race." Thinking suddenly of the second letter, Kathleen asked hopefully, "Are Uncle Razz and Aunt Mary and the baby coming too?"

"No, darlin'," said Mama. "But Razz did have exciting news. You know that piece of timber I told you Uncle Jeremiah bought for back taxes?"

19

"In Dry Grove?"

"Yes, that's the piece."

Dry Grove, a grove of trees north of the little village of Shirley, Illinois, was Mama's birthplace. She got a sigh in her voice every time she mentioned it. But it was too far away and too foreign-sounding to seem real to Kathleen. *No mountains? No cactus? Trees so thick they blocked out the sky?* Kathleen shivered at the thought.

"Jere asked Razz if he'd like to try his hand at making maple syrup there in the timber. It's the same piece of ground we lived on when we were children," Mama chattered on. "The house is pretty run-down, Razz says. Still, he's beside himself, rejoicing. Jere knew as much when he made the offer. He's turning into a fine young man, Jere is. You remember him, don't you, darlin'? He stopped by here on his way to see his half-brother Bryce out in California a couple years ago."

Kathleen remembered all right. Young and handsome and very polite, holding chairs and doors for her and Mama, saying "Excuse me," when he left the table and "I beg your pardon," when he didn't quite hear what was being said. But mostly what she remembered was that Jeremiah Bishop wasn't a blood relative. He'd been orphaned as a child. Gram Sophie had taken him in to raise, the same as she'd done for Mama. Not that Gram Sophie and Grandpa Dave thought any less of Mama and Uncle Jere. No sir, they were just as proud of them as they were of Gram Sophie's birth daughter, Aunt Maggie.

"I remember the first time I set eyes on Jeremiah," Mama was saying. "Depression was on, and here came Bryce Bishop to drop Jere on our doorstep. Bryce was certainly old enough to look after Jere himself, but Sophie never expected him to live up to the responsibility. Poor Jere. Just six years old, both parents gone and a brother who didn't want to be bothered. 'Course, all I saw at the time was this little boy dressed up like a prince and Sophie going all soft over him. He had a loose tooth and the first chance I got, I tied a string to a doorknob and jerked that tooth sideways. Sophie had to finish the job. She wasn't too happy with me.''

Kathleen giggled and pinched a chain in her paper straw. Mama, humming like a teapot, looking forward to company coming. If Kathleen didn't know better, she'd think she'd forgotten all about the day's bad news. A wonder, what letters from loved ones could do.

Four

The upgraded prospector's cabin Fawn Leroy called home was west of the jail, well off the road. Beyond the cabin, the terrain began leveling off from buttes and spires and mountain grandeur, rolling down toward the Mohave Valley.

Kathleen craned her neck as they cut across the jail yard. "I don't see any sign of a burro, do you?"

"It'd be out back," reasoned Binky.

A paloverde tree stood watch in front of the house. Some rocks of fair size were arranged around what looked like a cactus garden. But it was hard to spy undetected as there weren't any homes near Fawn's. It would be a long hot walk, if they were to circle around to the back undetected. Energy lagging, Kathleen had second thoughts concerning the secrecy of their quest. "I guess it'd be all right if you went to the door and asked Fawn outright if Captain Slade got her a burro."

Openly reluctant, Binky asked, "Why me?"

"Because you're the one needs to know. Whether

Fawn does or doesn't, I'm racing," Kathleen pointed out.

"I liked your first idea better. About circling around back and looking for ourselves, I mean."

"Are you sure? It's awful hot."

Binky kicked at a loose pebble. "What if her mother comes to the door?"

"So what if she does?"

"I don't think she likes me much."

Kathleen knew just how he felt. She had a feeling Fawn's mama didn't like her either. "Guess we'll just have to go around back, then."

They circled until they were out of sight of the Leroy cabin, then crossed a well-beaten track that led right to Fawn's back door. A less-traveled trail crept up the barren slope. Mindful of wind-borne cactus spines, Kathleen was careful where she put her hands as she crouched behind a pile of stones and spied on Fawn's backyard. There was a wash shed. A laundry bench, several clotheslines, a garbage barrel, and Fawn's mama's blue Plymouth. The weeds had been pulled, the bare yard swept clean, leaving nothing but some potted red flowers.

Binky shaded his eyes. "I don't see a burro, do you?"

"Either Richie was wrong, or Captain Slade hasn't brought it yet."

"Maybe he hasn't had time."

"Let's check back tomorrow."

Kathleen tipped back her cowboy hat and wiped her brow dry. "If I was you, I'd go ahead and enter Princess."

"And have Fawn rub it in when she beats me? No thanks."

"Well, Fawn's not going to keep me out. I'm going to make my own luck," said Kathleen.

"Not me. I'm waiting to see."

Kathleen's mouth tasted like chalk. She dusted the seat of her pants. "Let's go back."

They skirted cactus and watched for snakes and gila monsters along the desolate hillside. Just as they approached the trail, a pickup truck left the highway and came toward them on the trail. It kicked up dust as it rattled past them.

"Hey, that's Cookie. Wonder where he's headed?"

"Prospecting, probably."

There was still gold in the mountains. A lot of folks believed the mines would open again some day. Kathleen waited, expecting another glimpse of Cookie's truck as it worked through the hills. But it never came. She turned and started back the way they'd come.

"Where you going?" Binky hollered.

"Let's see about Cookie. He took off early today and he wouldn't say why."

They backtracked to their pile of rocks. Cookie'd parked his truck right next to Mrs. Leroy's blue Plymouth and was climbing out. Kathleen clamped her hands on her hips. "I'll be!"

"Maybe he brought his wash," suggested Binky.

Possibly. Mrs. Leroy's husband had been killed in a train accident shortly before she and Fawn moved to Oatman. She supported herself and Fawn sewing and doing laundry for folks who couldn't do for themselves. Widowers and single fellows, mostly. But Cookie wasn't toting wash. No sir. From where Kathleen stood, it looked like he had a handful of flowers. Mrs. Leroy came out to meet him. She was wearing a white dress with thin straps and a full skirt. With her yellow hair curling loosely about her shoulders, she looked almost as much a paper doll as Fawn. Kathleen watched as she took the flowers, turned, and led the way inside.

Binky grimaced. "Flowers!"

"Must have gone clear to Kingman to get them. I saw him heading out of town earlier."

"What'd he do that for?"

Kathleen twisted her mouth to one side, disliking the most obvious of reasons. "I don't know. Unless he's sweet on her."

Losing interest fast, Binky licked sun-chapped lips. "I'm thirsty. Let's start back."

But Kathleen resisted the demands of a dry throat and held out a few more minutes. Sure enough, Cookie and Mrs. Leroy and Fawn came parading out again. Fawn walked between them, holding Cookie's hand and telling him something that made him laugh. He said something in return, something that made *her* laugh. Then he patted her golden head and stooped down to tie her shoe. He'd never shown Kathleen half so much attention! Fawn got treated special at school, too, just because she was so prissy sweet. It was all an act, of course. The real Fawn Leroy was cutthroat in everything from marbles to spelling bees. Kids ignored her at school, and nobody wanted her over to play. That was why she had to tag along on her mama's date. Or so Kathleen reasoned as the three of them got into the truck and drove away.

On the way back through town, Binky stopped by Doolittle's Service Station. Ordinarily, business was brisk. But today, the drive was empty. There was no

25

one in sight. Kathleen's mood dampened as she remembered the new road and the silence in her daddy.

Binky jumped on the bell. Luke Doolittle's round face appeared at the window. Seeing it was only his little brother, he hollered, "Go away. We don't want any."

"We're thirsty. We need change for the pop machine," Binky hollered back.

"I'm not your piggy bank."

"Please? I'll pay you back," Binky whined like a squeaky wheel.

Luke leaned in the open door and gestured toward the machine. "There's no pop. I just emptied it."

"Aw, quit teasing."

"Look, if you don't believe me . . ."

Kathleen knew how this game went. They'd look. It'd be full of pop and Luke'd laugh at having suckered them. Then Binky would get all red-faced and ram his head into his brother's belly. From there on out, it was anyone's guess. She touched Binky's arm. "That's okay, Binky. Mama'll let us make Kool-Aid."

"Binky and Twinky, the Kool-Aid kids," Luke teased as the Doolittles' old tow truck rattled onto the drive. Binky's other brother Darrell climbed out, lugging several empty crates.

"Hey Twinky! I just told a sweet-toothed coyote you'd left town. Guess that means I saved your life, huh?" Darrell grinned and shoved a box at her. "Show some gratitude and start packing everything off the shelves inside.

"Packing?" yelped Binky. "What's going on?"

Darrell rolled his eyes. "Where you been, kid? The new road's opened. We're closing up."

"But not right away. Are we?" Binky's confidence

26

faltered. "I thought Dad said he'd give it a chance, see how things went once the rerouting opened."

"Didn't take him long to see," said Luke. "We haven't had a customer in hours."

For the second time that day, Binky went pale. Kathleen wasn't feeling so good either. She pressed closer. "So what're you going to do?"

"Move to Kingman. There's a fella down there with a gas station, all set to retire. He's hired Dad to manage his station."

Binky's jaw dropped. "Just like that? Why didn't somebody tell me?"

"Yeah, why didn't you?" Kathleen took Binky's part.

Darrell said something about Dad not wanting to build false hopes in case the job fell through. But that wasn't what Binky was asking at all.

"What about Princess?"

"Turn her out in the desert," said Darrell. "She can take care of herself."

"But she trusts people! What if somebody shoots her? What if they *eat* her? No sir, I'm not going anywhere," Binky declared. "I'm staying right here with Princess."

The older Doolittle brothers exchanged a wordless glance. Darrell draped an arm across his little brother's shoulder and said with uncustomary kindness, "Take it easy, Bink. You can come back and see Princess. Kingman's not far."

"You'll like Kingman," Luke took his cue from Darrell. "Just think, you can join Boy Scouts and all kinds of nifty stuff."

"Maybe Dad'll let you get a dog," said Darrell.

27

"And there's lots of kids. Some of 'em just as spunky as Twinky, I bet."

Binky clamped his hands over his ears and hissed through the space in his teeth, "Shut up! Both of you, shut up! We're not moving! You're jest making a stupid joke!"

Kathleen shot his brothers an accusing glance. But for once, they weren't laughing. Bad as she wanted them to be teasing, she knew they weren't. First 66, now Binky. The anxiety that'd been quietly building for months landed its second blow of the day.

Five

***

Binky and his family moved the next day. Five more gas stations closed their doors and a tourist court, too. The Pin and Curl, Richie's mama's beauty shop, vacated the following week. While Richie hadn't been as good a friend as Binky, Kathleen regretted the loss— particularly when students were dwindling at school like seats in a game of musical chairs. There were whispers that the doors would soon close and those who were left would be bussed to Mohave Valley.

Mama said it was almost like a storm had ripped through town, tearing it apart. Solomon Sal agreed, pointing out the need for those who remained to put aside their differences and work at salvaging what was left. Convincing herself that's what she had in mind, Kathleen made an overture of friendship toward Fawn one noon as they settled down to sack lunches.

"Are you getting a burro?" she asked.

Fawn's delicate, pink-tipped fingers paused in peeling her orange. She turned a glinty look on Kathleen. "Are you the one who's spreading that around?"

"No. I heard it, that's all," said Kathleen.

"Well, you better not be. Burros are loud and they're dirty and I wouldn't have one if it came with baton-twirling lessons. So there!"

Kathleen decided Solomon Sal's salvaging idea was for the birds. She walked home, even though Mama'd put a nice slice of pie in her lunch. It wasn't just Fawn's snippiness. Business had fallen off so at the restaurant, she hated leaving for fear she'd return from school to find her family packing. Mama didn't even look surprised to see her. Maybe she understood her need to see business going on as usual.

Cookie quit the next morning. Daddy said he did it out of kindness. But Kathleen couldn't help feeling a little hurt that in the days that followed he spent a lot of time with Mrs. Leroy and Fawn and yet never once came into Cactus Jack's to see how *they* were getting along. Mama upheld him, saying he was probably trying to avoid the third degree from the coffee cuppers. Their tongues were wagging on the subject of his dating the Captain's sister, sure enough.

But the fate of the town seemed to be producing the most rumors these days. With the mine company owning the land occupied by the town, the water, and a good many of the buildings as well, speculation about the mines reopening was a favored topic. It would mean new jobs. But some of the coffee cuppers claimed top brass in the mining company planned to turn the town into a mountain retreat for artists and writers and musicians. And still others were convinced they hoped to hire out Oatman as a Hollywood set for moviemaking. Mama scolded when she caught Kathleen eavesdropping on the coffee drinkers. But Kathleen listened anyway and crawled into bed each night picking through the rumors like a wish book.

The only good thing to come of lagging business was that it gave Kathleen more free time. She spent most of it racing Biscuit against the other pet burros in town. Some were younger than Biscuit but none so even-tempered and eager to please. Kathleen won every race. Her only real competition appeared to be the rumored prize-winning burro from a nearby ranch. So far, there'd been no sign of it. But the possibility nagged at Kathleen as she helped Daddy spruce up Cactus Jack's for Gram and Grandpa's visit and for the festivities. They worked steadily at whitewashing the front of the building, scraping gum off the boardwalk, and shining all the windows. One evening, Kathleen'd just come in from pulling the weeds around Biscuit's pen when Captain Slade strode into the restaurant and stradled a counter stool.

"Cup of coffee, Mrs. Fanta, and a word when you get time," he said.

It wasn't often Captain Slade came into the restaurant. Kathleen sidled up to the counter, planning to settle the matter once and for all. "Captain Slade, did you see last year's burro race over the mountains?"

"I sure did." Stale cigar smoke overpowered the smell of beer and hair cream as the Captain swept off his hat and reached for an ashtray.

"Do you happen to recall who won?" she eased into the burning question.

"A ranch hand by the name of . . ."

"I meant the burro," Kathleen interrupted.

"Yes I do. How about you? Can you name the

31

burro?'' The Captain peeled the wrapping off a fresh cigar as he awaited her reply.

"No. The reason I'm asking is I heard . . .''

"Kathleen!'' Mama turned sharply, the coffee pot in hand.

"Yes, Mama?''

"Take the ketchup bottles back to the kitchen and wipe them clean, please.''

Kathleen sighed and turned away, discouraged at how hard it was to learn the simple truth. She took her time gathering bottles, watching out of the corner of her eye as Mama poured Captain a cup.

"Just checking in to see if you folks are giving any thought to selling out,'' said the Captain to her mother.

Kathleen's heart leaped to her throat. Though Mama's reply was too quiet for her to catch, it opened the door to negotiations, for Captain Slade proceeded to make an offer. Mama recoiled as if a snake had jumped out of his hat.

"That's a fraction of what we gave for the place!''

"Well now, Mrs. Fanta, don't get your dander up. You got to stop and consider that the business climate here in Oatman has all but dried up.''

"If you're getting something to eat, I'll take your order. Otherwise, I've got work waiting in the kitchen,'' said Mama.

"This'll do.'' The Captain stirred cream into his coffee.

Mama clattered off with a tub of dirty dishes. As soon as she was gone from sight, Captain Slade slid a quarter under his saucer and left without taking a sip. Kathleen carried her tray of ketchup bottles back to the kitchen and parked them on the battered worktop.

"Just plain insulting! I'd sooner burn the place than let it go that cheap," Mama fumed.

"Want me to get Daddy?"

"Don't be silly, I'm fine," claimed Mama. But she was wearing the pattern off the dishes with her scrubbing.

It wasn't long before Daddy strolled in from the desert. He showed Kathleen a button he'd found from an old cavalry uniform. Mama didn't pay the least heed. She related Captain Slade's visit in a burst of indignation. "He's a bald-faced opportunist, that's what he is!" she concluded.

The serenity of a desert sunset melted from Daddy's face. His hands fluttered like birds with no place to light. Scratching his chin. Rubbing his eye. Turning his hat in his hand.

Kathleen felt as if invisible hands were choking off her breath. "Are we selling?" she blurted.

"Not at that price," said Daddy.

Mama slid him a look and he clammed right up. "We're about done here, Kathleen," she said. "It's been a warm day. Why don't you run and check on Biscuit's water?"

"Where would we go if we had to close up?" Kathleen refused to be so easily dismissed.

Daddy transferred his hat to her head and tipped up her chin. "Until we tell you otherwise, Oatman's our home. Fair enough?"

"Okay," she whispered, but the tremor in his hand was less than reassuring.

Mama turned back to the sink, all prickly spined. Jerking at the faucet. Making the dishes clatter in the sink. Kathleen crept soundlessly past the storeroom and

33

paused on the threshold of the parlor. She stood at the door a moment and heard their voices start up over the nervous tap-tapping of Daddy's feet.

"We're going to have to make a decision, Russell."

"No point in rushing into anything."

"If you're set on staying, I could speak to Myrt Myers. She says there's an opening at the State Inspection Station where her son works. It'd mean moving to Kingman, but . . ."

"I don't need you finding a job for me," Daddy cut her short.

Kathleen backed away from the door, stomach cramping. Would they have to move to Kingman? What about Biscuit? She could never leave him behind!

Six

———◆———

The thought of Biscuit carried Kathleen out the back door. She attached reins to his halter, flung a leg over, and leaned to one side to open the gate. He lumbered surefooted down the alley to Solomon Sal's. Miss Solomon's place was dark. Knowing her habits, Kathleen circled around to the front.

" 'Evening, Kathleen. Wasn't expecting you this late," her old friend called from the porch bench. "I was just thinking about your Daddy. I haven't seen him in a few days. He all right?"

"I guess."

"And your Mama? She still running herself ragged?"

It made Kathleen cross that Mama could even think about moving to Kingman. She looped Biscuit's reins around the hitching post and said shortly, "I've been helping. Anyway, it isn't like we're busy."

"Worry's more wearing than work." Solomon Sal fanned her face with her hat and patted the bench, motioning Kathleen to join her. "What's on your mind?"

Kathleen slumped beside her. She swung her feet,

boot soles whispering against the bare planks. "Mama's wanting Daddy to get a job in Kingman."

"With things so slow, it's reasonable to consider making a change."

"Are *you* thinking of leaving Oatman?"

Miss Solomon said, "Lord willing, the only move I'll be making this late in life is to glory land."

Ignoring Miss Solomon's reminder that she had no intentions of living forever, Kathleen hung her hopes on her first choice in rumors and ventured, "I'm praying the movie stars'll come. Then we'll have plenty of business."

"Movie stars?" Miss Solomon scratched her woolly white head. "Carole Lombard and Clark Gable honeymooned over there at the hotel. And Tom Mix came through town once. But far as I can tell, that's the last Oatman's seen of any movie stars."

"Yes, but they're saying the mining company plans to turn the whole town into a Hollywood set."

"They're also talking about artists overrunning the place and gold being mined from the mountains again, but I'm not paying much heed. 'The mouths of fools feed on foolishness,' don't you know," quoted Miss Solomon. "Best just to let the good Lord take care of things the way he sees fit."

Kathleen squirmed, the hard bench creasing the back of her legs. "Captain Slade came by and made Mama an offer on Cactus Jack's."

"He did, did he?"

"It was so low, Mama got mad and he left," Kathleen confided.

"Your folks deserve a fair price for the place. It's

looking real nice with that fresh coat of paint. Did you do that?'' asked Miss Solomon.

"Daddy helped.'' Kathleen stopped short, wondering suddenly if she'd been working so hard after school to make the place look good for a buyer rather than for Gram and Grandpa and the Jubilee. If so she'd been working against her own interests! Feeling tricked, she sputtered, "I hope nobody wants Cactus Jack's. Then we'll get to stay.''

"Don't be wishing hard luck on your parents, child,'' Miss Solomon chided. "If they're thinking of selling, it's out of necessity.''

"But it isn't fair!''

"Whoever said life was fair was just pulling your leg.'' Solomon Sal hugged her a long moment, then let her go, asking, "Do your folks know you're here?''

Kathleen wagged her head no.

"Better start home then, before they get anxious.''

Kathleen said good-bye and took the empty street home. Biscuit's water bucket was nearly empty. She picked it up and surprised a tarantula hiding beneath it. It was just coming awake for the night and was slow to move. Quickly, Kathleen overturned the bucket and trapped the spider.

Mama was talking on the phone when Kathleen raced into the restaurant for a jar. Hand over the mouthpiece, Mama asked, "Where've you been?''

"Miss Solomon's. I caught something. I need a jar.''

"There's some salad dressing jars in the storeroom. What'd you catch?''

"A tarantula.''

Mama grimaced. "Darlin', I don't know about your keeping a spider.''

"I'll keep him under the sink. You won't even have to look if you're scared."

Mama let her tone pass, and offered the phone. "Say hello to Gram Sophie."

Her grandparents' upcoming visit was a welcome distraction from the day's news. Kathleen took the phone gladly. "Hi, Gram. When are you coming?"

"Hello, sweet one," said Gram, her voice strong and warm and loving. "We'll be there on Sunday—that's Columbus Day—and guess who we're bringing?"

"Columbus?"

Gram chuckled. "No, darlin'. Your cousin Charlie is coming along with us."

Charlie'd come once before several years ago and they'd had great fun. Delighted, Kathleen asked, "What about school?"

"His teacher sent his books and his assignments along. Rob and Maggie drove him here from Missouri yesterday and spent the night with us. Sure was good to see them."

"Tell Charlie I've got a spider trapped outside. It's big as my hand. I'll keep it till he gets here so he can see it."

"My!" exclaimed Gram.

"Mama told you about the Jubilee, didn't she? And that I'm riding Biscuit in a race down 66?"

"Spiders and burros for pets and a race right down a highway?" Gram chuckled. "Now why should that surprise me? Your mama was always fearless, too."

Kathleen was pleased at sharing a trait with Mama, even if she was miffed at Mama's Kingman suggestion. Besides, it was hard to stay glum with Charlie coming. He had spark and imagination and a nice temperament.

Humming over the success of her Columbus joke, the glow of making Gram laugh, and the joy of company on the way, Kathleen passed back the phone to Mama and went for a salad dressing jar to imprison her spider.

Seven

The restaurant was closed on Sunday for church and for rest and "for family", as Mama put it. After lunch, Daddy dozed behind the weekly newspaper while Mama sat with her mending. She gave Kathleen a scrap of red cloth and showed her how to make a hatband out of it for Biscuit's straw hat. Kathleen's stitches weren't small and neat like Mama's, but the band looked pretty good once she'd tacked it to Biscuit's hat.

"My, don't you look nice!" Kathleen grinned as Biscuit stretched his neck and showed his teeth. Encouraged by his vanity, she brushed his coat until it gleamed. Some boot black did wonders for his hooves. But cleaning his teeth proved tedious, as Biscuit's main interest was in eating the toothpaste.

It was suppertime when Kathleen finished Biscuit's grooming and their company still hadn't arrived. Kathleen wandered around front and nearly careened into Old Coot.

"Dad-blame it, young 'un! Don't you ever watch where yer goin'?" he complained.

40

"Sorry, Mr. Coot. I was looking for cars."

"Cars? I thought you was a burro girl."

"I am. But my grandparents are coming for a visit and they're bringing my cousin."

"That so?" He coughed and cleared his throat and spat toward the street. "You about ready for the race on Saturday?"

"I've been practicing."

"That-a-girl! I've got a double eagle ridin' on you."

"The race is just for fun. It isn't for betting."

"Mind yer manners," he snapped. "Confounded young 'uns, sassing their elders."

Kathleen squeezed back a grin.

Old Coot scratched his whiskery chin. "You know, don't ya, that burros ain't so much stubborn as cautious? They ain't gonna rush over uncertain ground unless they trust their rider. That's why I'm leanin' toward you. Ya got a good friendship with that burro of yers."

"We'll do our best," Kathleen promised.

"Blister yer hide if you don't," he grunted.

"Yessir." Kathleen watched the darkness swallow him up as he ambled on home to his sheepherder's wagon. Gruff was an odd way of being friendly, but it appeared Old Coot knew no other.

She stepped back inside and was about to pull the blinds when the door opened and a man strode in. His hat shadowed his face and he kept his head down as he asked, "Is this a good place to eat?"

Kathleen's heartbeat quickened. Her gaze raced to the full-figured woman who followed him in. "Quit your teasing, Dave, and give our granddaughter a hug."

"Gram! I knew it was him all along!"

Lilac water, face powder, and laughter sweetened

41

Gram's hug. Grandpa hugged Kathleen too, then he turned and drew a sleepy-eyed Charlie through the door. He'd grown a lot since Kathleen'd seen him last. But his eyes twinkled like she remembered and his hair was as dark as a freshly tarred road. Her gaze shifted to the "I Like Ike" campaign button on his shirt and the three gold pins beneath it.

"What're these?" she asked.

Charlie tucked his chin and looked down. "For perfect attendance."

"All three of them?"

He nodded.

"At school?" She cocked her head and grinned.

He grinned too, venturing, "I guess I won't be getting one this year."

Mama came running, face glowing like a Christmas star. Grandpa and Gram tangled limbs, hugging her at the very same time. Daddy trailed behind. He shook Grandpa's hand and kissed Gram's cheek. They all talked at once, voices spilling one over the other.

"How was the trip?"

"Two flat tires and an overheated radiator."

"We've been watching a while, and thinking you might wait till morning."

"Probably should have. Land, what a mountain!"

"Like scaling the threads on a screw!"

"You must be exhausted. Are you hungry? Sit down while I fix you something to eat."

Kathleen turned the lock on the door and pulled the blinds. The reunion continued over the best leftovers Cactus Jack's had to offer. Even Daddy relaxed and enjoyed himself. Instead of heading out for his solitary after-supper walk, he brought out the desert relics he'd acquired over time. While Gram and Grandpa admired his collection, Kathleen took Charlie out back to renew acquaintance with Biscuit.

Proud of what a fine picture he made, she confided, "Biscuit and I have been practicing for the race after school everyday. Our chances of winning are real good unless Fawn Leroy's uncle shows up with a burro for her to race."

"Who's Fawn Leroy?" he asked.

"A snippy girl in my class at school."

Charlie scratched Biscuit behind the ears. "I came in second once, in a bicycle race."

"What kind of bicycle do you have?"

"A big red Schwinn. It's Nick's. But he lets me use it. He's bought a truck now that he's working for Mr. Phillips laying bricks. How about you? Do you have a bicycle?"

Kathleen shook her head no. Her fingers skipped lightly over Biscuit's ears.

"Guess you don't need one, with Biscuit around."

Biscuit rolled back his lips, tossed his head, and brayed to the affirmative. Kathleen and Charlie both laughed.

Charlie patted Biscuit's neck. "He should come in handy around the camp. Mama says they get a lot of snow there in the wintertime. I wonder, has he ever seen snow?"

Puzzled, Kathleen echoed, "Snow?"

Charlie nodded. "He *is* going with you to the syrup camp, isn't he?"

"Syrup camp? You mean at Uncle Razz's?"

"Right. In Illinois. That's where you're moving, isn't it?"

43

A smothering feeling closed in on Kathleen. "'Course not," she said sharply. "Where'd you get such an idea?"

Charlie met her gaze for a moment then abruptly changed the subject. "Gram says you don't have school tomorrow on account of Columbus Day falling on Sunday. You want to go riding or something?"

Kathleen's thoughts raced. She remembered Uncle Razz's letter about running a syrup camp. Had he invited them to come help run it? That was crazy! Daddy didn't know anything about making syrup. And yet . . . "Did Mama say we were going to Uncle Razz's?" she asked. Charlie was so slow to answer, Kathleen got right up in his face and repeated, "Did she?"

Reluctantly, he nodded yes.

Head reeling, Kathleen asked, "When?"

"Two days ago." Charlie shot a glance back over his shoulder. He whispered, "The house and the station are on the same party line. Mama and Dad had already headed back to Missouri, and I'd gone out to the station with Grandpa. I listened in." Charlie pinched a pleat in his trousers and said into her stunned silence, "I'm sorry I said anything. I thought you knew."

They were moving and not just to Kingman! Mama hadn't said a word! Daddy, either! Kathleen flew inside and raced upstairs to her room. She knocked a chair out of the way and slammed her door so hard, Biscuit's picture toppled off her chest of drawers. Footsteps sounded on the stairs.

"Kathleen?" Mama poked her head in the door. "What's all the noise up here?"

White spots danced before her eyes. They hissed and

44

spit and sizzled like grease on the grill. "Why didn't you tell me we were moving?"

Mama's eyebrows shot up. "Who told you that?"

"Are we?"

Mama leaned over and righted the chair. Carefully, she said, "We've lost nearly all of our business with the road changing. You can see that for yourself, Kathleen. Hard as we've tried, we can't make a go of it here any longer. We have to make a living."

"But not in Illinois! Daddy could get a job in Kingman if he has to. Like Binky's dad."

"Your daddy isn't like Binky's dad," said Mama. "He needs the kind of work he can walk away from if he has to."

"Daddy works hard," Kathleen said fiercely.

"Yes, darlin', he does. He works hard. But he works different. A lot of employers won't understand that he's best at being his own boss. But Razz will. The war changed him, too."

Kathleen clapped her hands over her ears. She refused to listen about a war she couldn't remember. Or about little things seeming big to Daddy and big things, insurmountable. It was Mama's way of shifting the blame for not telling her what they had in mind.

"You should have told me we were moving. Daddy promised he would!"

"Daddy and I didn't want to dampen Gram and Grandpa's visit for you." Mama caught her hands in her own, making her listen. "Or the Jubilee and the burro race. We aren't leaving in a rush like so many folks did. We're waiting for a buyer who'll pay what the place is worth."

45

"You still should have told me! You told Gram. Charlie heard on the phone. Everyone knew but me!"

Mama studied her from troubled eyes. "It wasn't an easy decision. We've both agonized over it."

"We're taking Biscuit with us, aren't we?"

"How, Kathleen? It's eighteen hundred miles!"

"We can't leave him behind! What if he got hurt? Who would take care of him?"

"Try not to worry, Kathleen. We'll think of a way to keep him safe." Mama retrieved the framed snapshot of Biscuit from the floor where it had fallen.

Kathleen snatched it from her and dragged a hand across burning eyes.

"I'm sorry, baby. I truly am." Mama sighed and moved away. She turned back at the door, saying, "Come on down when you get to feeling better and we'll talk some more."

Kathleen hugged her pet's picture to her heart as Mama's footsteps receded. *What good was talk? If they were moving, there wasn't a thing she could do. That battle was already lost. But she wouldn't give up Biscuit. No sir! Not ever! Mama would soon see about that!*

Eight

Kathleen slept poorly and awoke at dawn. Thought of the impending move jabbed like a hot poker. She dressed and went downstairs and glowered when Mama came at her with a spoonful of medicine.

"Open up, darlin'."

"It makes me gag."

Mama's morning fresh smile lost its cheery curve. "Just open your mouth, Kathleen, and get it over with."

Charlie was at the table, taking interest in the medicine show. Daddy, heading toward the restaurant, paused and looked back. His fingers drummed against his thighs as he waited for Kathleen to open her mouth. She let Mama spoon the wretched stuff in, then tried, as Daddy walked on, to pool it on a narrow patch of tongue. Every taste bud quivered. She shot for the back door.

"Swallow!" said Mama.

"Ah dee-ahd!"

Mama blocked her path, small and unyielding in her faded cotton robe. "Rose Kathleen Fanta, you're trying my patience! Swallow and be done with it!"

47

Kathleen gave in and swallowed. Gagged. Shuddered as the foul-tasting stuff offended all the way to her stomach.

"That's more like it. What's got into you, anyway?"

War had been declared, that's what! Kathleen leaned her head under the kitchen faucet, shot her mouth full of water, then darted out the back door and took malicious aim at Mama's precious peach tree. "I'd rather be puny than take that awful stuff! Short and puny with watery blood," she declared on her way back in.

"Iron-poor," corrected Mama. "You're a little anemic, that's all. And keep your voice down. You'll wake Gram and Grandpa."

"Ever try holding your nose when you swallow?" asked Charlie.

"Wouldn't help. Smell." Kathleen shoved the bottle of daily torment his way.

He sniffed and recoiled, eyes watering. *"Phew!* What's in it?"

"Bat droppings, most likely. And snake oil. She's trying to kill me."

"Someone got up on the wrong side of the bed," said Mama.

Charlie grinned as if they'd staged the whole thing for his entertainment.

"It's so nice having you here. Wish Maggie and Rob and Nick and Becca could have come, too. Remember what fun it was when you all came three years ago?" Mama patted his head, then started away.

"Charlie and me are going outside," Kathleen called after her.

"Eat some cereal first. Then make your bed and

48

gather the eggs.'' Mama closed herself in the bathroom to pretty herself up before opening the restaurant.

Charlie fingered the medicine bottle. He dropped his voice to a whisper. ''Do you think Biscuit would drink it?''

Kathleen blinked. ''Now why would you pull such a mean trick on Biscuit?''

Charlie brushed his hand over the top of his head. The cowlick Mama'd patted down stood at attention. ''I was thinking of the race,'' he explained. ''It might make him stronger. And faster.''

''He's plenty fast without it,'' said Kathleen.

Charlie shrugged. ''It was just a thought. It never hurts to have an edge.''

He made a good point. But if she should lose this battle, she didn't want Biscuit's last memories of her tainted by that vile-tasting medicine! Kathleen explained as much.

''Then you're at war with your mother?'' asked Charlie. ''Can you do that?''

''Course.'' Kathleen ate fast and sloshed water over her bowl before opening the cupboard beneath the sink.

''This is Harriet. I told you about her on the phone.'' She set the jar on the table.

Charlie's dark eyes widened as he peered through the glass. ''Spiders don't grow *nearly* that big in Missouri.''

''Mama doesn't like her either.'' Kathleen climbed up on the kitchen table and loosened the glass globe covering the light bulb.

''You're getting bugs in my cereal,'' Charlie observed.

''Fish them out. Harriet'll eat 'em.''

''Kathleen, get down from there.'' Mama stuck her

49

foot into her freshly polished shoe and marched across the kitchen, strings trailing. She swept Charlie's cereal away, saying in a much sweeter tone, "I'll get you a fresh bowl, Charlie."

"Never mind, Aunt Susan. I'm full."

Kathleen put the insects from the light globe into the salad dressing jar. Nocturnal by nature, Harriet was motionless this morning. Kathleen shook Harriet out of the jar, asking, "Want to hold her?"

Charlie skidded back in his chair. "No thanks."

"She's never bit me. Even if she did, her bite wouldn't be poison the way people think."

Charlie gave Harriet closer consideration. "She sure has hairy legs."

"Long, hairy legs. She's fast, too, when she's not groggy with sleep. She's nocturnal, you know. If she were to get loose at night . . ." Aware of Mama looking on, Kathleen left the sentence unfinished. She slid a piece of paper under the spider. "Guess what, Mama? I've decided if I can't take Biscuit to Illinois with me, then I'll take Harriet instead. She'll be my new pet." Paper in hand, she turned Harriet motionless upon it.

"Into the jar with the spider, Kathleen, or back to the wild. Take your choice," said Mama without so much as a grimace.

Disappointed in her lack of reaction, Kathleen put the spider away.

"Would you really keep a spider for a pet?" whispered Charlie, as they climbed the stairs.

"Not for long. But Mama doesn't need to know that." She explained what Mama'd said about leaving Biscuit behind.

New understanding dawned on Charlie's face. "So

you're hoping she'll change her mind and find a way,
rather 'n risk your keeping Harriet as a pet?''

Kathleen nodded, and he smiled in appreciation of
her strategy.

Gram and Grandpa were still sleeping. She and Charlie worked quietly, making their beds. By the time they
came back down, Mama'd gone into the restaurant.

Charlie helped feed the hens and gather the eggs and
measure out Biscuit's breakfast of alfalfa pellets.

"I had a bad dream about Cookie chasing Biscuit
with a bottle of ketchup and a carving knife," Kathleen
confided as she scooped the yard clean of chicken litter
and burro dung.

Charlie poured water into Biscuit's drinking bucket.
"Who's Cookie?"

"Wesley Wright. He used to be our cook. He quit
when the traffic stopped. It was just a dream. Cookie
wouldn't hurt Biscuit. Though someone else might,"
she revealed her worst fear. "Sometimes burros get poi-
soned if they're pesky. Or shot and turned into barbe-
cue." She shuddered.

"I'll help you think of a way to take him if I can,"
Charlie volunteered.

"Good," said Kathleen. She rinsed off the shovel and
leaned it against the chicken coop reminding, "Last
night you said something about using Biscuit at the
syrup camp. How would he be useful, do you think?''

"I've seen pictures of horses pulling sap tanks.
Maybe a burro would work just as well."

"He's strong. He'd work as hard as a horse. Maybe
harder. I'll tell Mama so," said Kathleen. "Though I
still don't know how we'd get him there."

"Do you have any friends who drive trucks across the country?" asked Charlie.

"Lots of truckers used to eat at Cactus Jack's. But that was before the road changed."

"Maybe you could borrow a horse trailer."

"Returning it would be a problem."

Charlie twisted his mouth to one side. "You'd have to buy it, I guess."

"How much would that cost?"

He shrugged. "I don't know."

"Daddy paid me three dollars for helping him paint. Plus, I have forty cents of my own."

"It'd be more than that, I think."

Kathleen looped her arms around Biscuit's neck and sighed. "I need a plan. A *good* plan."

"Can we ride Biscuit while we think?" asked Charlie.

Kathleen led Biscuit out the gate, stretched a hand down and pulled Charlie up behind her. Biscuit ambled up the street, passing beneath the big draping banner that announced Oatman's Jubilee on Saturday. Every store was flying the American flag, just like on the Fourth of July. The Mohave Miner, the weekly newspaper, had printed up posters announcing the schedule of events. They were mounted on every street corner.

"There's a car coming," Charlie warned as Biscuit strayed to the center of the street.

Kathleen looked back to see Captain Slade's big convertible slipping up on them. He had a backseat passenger with him. Curious, she turned Biscuit for a better look.

"It's a burro!" exclaimed Charlie.

Fawn's prize-winning burro? All the blood rushed to

Kathleen's head. Captain Slade stopped the car beside her.

"Remember the other day, you were asking about the winning burro in the Black Mountain race? Well, you're looking at her." He tipped his jaunty hat and swept a hand toward the sleek jenny. The dainty-looking critter was predominantly white with splotches of brown on her back.

"What's her name?" Charlie spoke from behind Kathleen.

"Patches."

Disinterested in the introduction, Patches leaned over the seat and plucked a cigar right out of Captain Slade's pocket.

"Give that back! You're no good for racing if you're sick!" The Captain turned in the seat and tried unsuccessfully to retrieve the cigar.

"She's going to eat it, paper and all," warned Charlie.

"Be a good girl, now," pleaded the Captain. He opened the door, folded the front seat forward, and climbed in back to wrestle the cigar away. Patches wheeled, hooves flashing in the sunlight. Captain Slade leaped over the side of the car to avoid getting clipped. The burro stepped out the yawning door and set off up the street. Captain scrambled after her. He got in front of her, waved his arms, and tried to turn her back.

"Whoa, there. Around you go! Whoa, I say!"

The burro looked right at the Captain and sucked up the cigar like a Hoover sweeper. Kathleen giggled and Charlie grinned, too.

"You've had your fun. Now back you go," growled the Captain. He caught the little burro by the halter.

Patches turned and ambled toward the children, sweet as pie. She stayed close to the curb all the way back to the car. But she stopped just short of the faded white stripe at the highway's edge.

"Get the car door, would you, son?" Captain Slade called to Charlie.

Charlie slid off Biscuit and held the car door open. Captain slipped his hand through Patches's halter and tugged. The jenny backed away, refusing to climb in. The Captain struggled with the willful burro, his face growing shiny, his shaving lotion pungent in the morning sun. But no matter how hard he worked, cajoled, and threatened, he couldn't get Patches into the car.

"How about you and the boy pull on her halter, and I'll push?" he asked.

Push? It didn't seem like a safe idea to Kathleen. She was suddenly aware of Old Coot watching from the sidewalk.

"Go on, young 'uns, give it a try," he urged, a devilish gleam in his eye.

Kathleen shrugged and slid off Biscuit's back. She and Charlie got on each side of Patches, gripping her halter. They pulled while the Captain pushed at the jenny's rump, huffing and sweating and swearing beneath his breath. The dainty burro flattened her ears and skidded sideways rather than edge any closer to the Captain's car.

"She's afeared of the line," Old Coot called. "She's got no depth perception."

"Is that so? Then how is it she climbed out of the car without hesitation?" snapped the Captain.

Old Coot clamped his jaw shut and offered nothing

further. Kathleen and Charlie kept tugging until finally Captain Slade was forced to admit defeat.

"There's a quarter in it for you, girlie, if you'll crawl on this burro and follow me down the road."

The Captain smiled, showing the teeth Old Coot had paid for. But Kathleen couldn't think of a single reason for doing him a favor. She was about to refuse when from the walk, Old Coot's hand shot up in a covert gesture. He was wanting her to gouge the Captain in the wallet. Reminded of her need for cash, she beamed at the Captain and said, "Make it a dollar and you've got a deal."

Nine

The Captain attached leather reins to the halter. He held Patches's head as Kathleen mounted. "You can handle her, can't you?"

"Of course I can." Eager to add the promised fee to her horse trailer fund, Kathleen looked back to see Charlie mounting Biscuit. He nudged Biscuit with his heels and pulled up even with her.

The Captain got in his car and crept on down the road, leaving Kathleen and Charlie to follow. Patches broke into a willing amble. Unlike Biscuit, she stayed to the side of the road, never once straying over the white line.

They continued through town, then turned up the dusty back trail Kathleen and Binky had used not long ago. Along the way, Kathleen told Charlie a little more about Fawn Leroy, emphasizing her love of winning and her dislike of burros.

The Captain parked at the edge of Fawn Leroy's backyard. Patches stopped short of the sheets hanging on Mrs. Leroy's lines. Their billowing made her skitterish.

"Whoa, there. Easy," crooned Kathleen, knees locking around the burro's round belly. Patches had just settled down when the Captain tooted the car horn. She jumped so violently, she nearly unseated Kathleen.

"There, there. Pretty baby," Kathleen soothed, regaining control once more.

"Gwen? Fawn? Anybody home?" hollered the Captain.

Mrs. Leroy's car was gone. But Fawn was home. She pranced out the door, twirling a baton. "Uncle Batch, watch this!" She pitched the baton in the air. It made a silver arc, then came down and glanced off her nose. She winced and rubbed her snout. "Oops. Wait a second. Are you watching?" She flung it once more. Squinting, grabbing, missing.

"Bravo!" cheered the Captain, just like she'd planned to hit herself in the eye.

Kathleen grinned at Charlie. He didn't even respond, he was staring so. She looked back at Fawn. Her mama must have made her baton-twirling dress. It was short. It was red. It was trimmed out in fringe and glittery sequins, and it shimmered in the sunlight just like her golden hair. But her nose wasn't bleeding. And her eye wasn't swelling. That left only one reason for Charlie's gaping.

Charlie slid off Biscuit's back and walked toward Fawn. Politely, he offered, "I can show you if you like."

"Who are you?" she asked cautiously.

"Charlie Kelsey." He smoothed down his spikey hair, shook her hand, and reached for the baton. "May I?"

Fawn relinquished the baton and stood with arms

57

crossed, foot tapping. Charlie dried first one hand then the other on his pants, then he set the baton to twirling. Looking on, Kathleen's surprise gave way to cousinly pride. Charlie picked up his feet, twirling and marching as grandly as if a whole parade followed.

"Wow!" Fawn's eyes shone with envy. "Where'd you learn that?"

"My sister Becca is a majorette. She and her friends practice in our yard all the time," said Charlie.

"And they taught you? What all did they teach you?"

Charlie whirled the baton over his head. He moved his legs like scissors, twirling the silver stick between them. He pitched it into the air, caught it, tossed it again, turned and caught it behind his back.

"Bravo!" called the Captain, this time in earnest.

Fawn clapped and cheered. "You're *terrific!*"

"He's my cousin," said Kathleen.

Fawn's eyes narrowed as she acknowledged Kathleen's presence. "What're *you* doing here?"

"She's delivering a present." Captain Slade motioned for Kathleen to climb down. "Where's your mama?"

"Picking up laundry. She should be back right away." Fawn twisted on one foot, and asked demurely, "Is the present for me, Uncle Batch?"

"You bet. Right there she is! What do you think?" Captain Slade swept an arm toward Patches.

Fawn's face fell like a ton of hard rock.

"Isn't she a beaut? Sturdy legs, nice strong back, slender neck," said the Captain, circling the jenny as he sang her praises. "Best of all, she runs like there's bees on her tail. You're a cinch to win the burro race on this little lady. Come on over here, Sunshine, and I'll give you a leg up."

58

Fawn looked as if she'd taken one too many hits from the baton. Eager as Kathleen was to steal Charlie away from the scene of infatuation, this was just too good to miss.

"She's spirited. You'll want to hang on tight," Kathleen offered innocently.

Fawn's face turned as bright as her dress. But she stuck her chin in the air and admitted, "I'm scared, Uncle Batch. I've never been on a donkey before."

"There's nothing to it, Sunshine. I'll walk you through it."

"I'll help."

"Charlie!" protested Kathleen. "You hardly know how yourself."

"We'll learn together. It'll be fun."

"Yes, Charlie. Stay," Fawn beamed at him. "I want you to teach me how to catch the baton."

"The race is Saturday," the Captain reminded. "You'd better spend your time learning to ride."

"Maybe we can do both," said Charlie.

Offended he'd chosen snippy Fawn over his own cousin, Kathleen reminded, "Mama doesn't know where we are."

"Ask permission and come back. Please, Charlie?" Fawn underscored who she was inviting.

"I'll stay. Gram won't care," said Charlie.

"Go ahead, then. See if I care." Chin in the air, Kathleen climbed aboard Biscuit, then wheeled around to ask the Captain, "Where's my dollar?"

Captain Slade pulled out his wallet, scanned it briefly, then put it back in his pocket. "I seem to be out of small bills. I'll drop by Cactus Jack's later and pay you."

Kathleen headed out, then glanced back, hoping Charlie'd change his mind. What she saw instead was Fawn making a face at her. Glowering, she returned the sentiment, and rode home alone.

Mama and Gram were in the restaurant kitchen. Mama looked up from turning an egg on the grill. "Where's Charlie?" she asked.

"Fawn Leroy's house."

"What's he doing out there?"

"Baton twirling and burro riding and anything else Fawn wants him to." Kathleen flounced to the sink for a drink.

"I thought you didn't like Fawn," said Mama.

"I don't."

"Then what prompted you to go out to her house?" asked Mama, sliding eggs onto a plate.

Kathleen bent a knee, piled one scuffed boot on top of the other, and explained how it had transpired.

"Is Charlie somewhere he doesn't belong?" asked Gram when she fell silent.

"He's fine, Sophie. Kathleen's just never had much in common with Fawn. But there's no reason Charlie and Fawn can't be friends."

"He's *my* cousin, not hers," protested Kathleen.

Neither Mama nor Gram commented. Sipping her water, watching Gram dish fried potatoes onto the plate with the eggs, she asked, "How much does a horse trailer cost, Gram?"

"I wouldn't have any idea, dear."

"Bet Mama could buy me one if she wanted to."

"Run wash your hands and tell Grandpa to come have some breakfast." Mama declined to defend herself.

Kathleen shuffled away. In the corridor off the storeroom, just out of sight, she heard Mama say, "Kathleen has her heart set on taking Biscuit when we go."

"I see," said Gram.

"Even if we had a horse trailer, it'd be an ordeal," said Mama.

"It'd slow you down, that's for sure. Though I reckon it's more than the burro worrying the child," ventured Gram.

"I know." Mama sighed. A knife whispered through toast. "This is the only home she's ever known."

"Uprooting is never easy. You know that first hand," said Gram. " 'Course you left more than a burro behind. Have you talked to her about that?"

"She's in no mood to hear it," said Mama.

"Tell her anyway. Might take some of the vinegar out of her. Not that it's any of my business," Gram added hastily.

"And you always were one for tending your own knitting, weren't you?"

"Then I *am* getting meddlesome?" Gram clucked her tongue. "Next, you'll be calling me Greer Tims."

"Greer Tims!" Mama laughed.

"Suker, she's a good child fighting disappointment, that's all. I wasn't criticizing."

"Greer Tims," Mama repeated, just like she hadn't kept up with the conversation. "Took me years to realize she meant well. When Kathleen was born, I found myself thinking of her and how she used to tell me my name meant "lily". She was forever prodding me to live up to that kind of purity."

"Miss Tims was one for names, all right," said Gram.

"Did I ever tell you the meaning of 'Kathleen'?" asked Mama.

"I don't guess I ever stopped to wonder," confessed Gram.

"Purity," said Mama. "I bought a little name book at the dime store just before she was born. When I read that, I knew right then if I had a girl, I'd name her Kathleen."

"I reckon Miss Tims'd be pleased," said Gram.

Kathleen knew about their names sharing a similar meaning. It was the pride in Mama's voice, the pleasure she'd taken in choosing a name that caught her up short. Since her feet hit the floor at daybreak, she hadn't given Mama much to pleasure in. *It was Mama's own fault, though. How could she expect her to give up Biscuit without a fight?*

But it could be that staying mad at Mama until she gave in wasn't the best way of getting her way. Spiders and tantrums and sulks mightn't work either. Just what would it take to change Mama's mind? Gram's mention of vinegar sent one of Solomon Sal's quotes echoing through Kathleen's head: "You can catch more flies with honey than vinegar."

The question was, could you keep a burro by being sweet?

Ten

———◆———

Kathleen found Grandpa at the kitchen sink with his face all lathered up. "Grandpa, who's Greer Tims?"

"A maiden lady. Lived next door to us when your Mama was about your size. Why do you ask?"

"Gram and Mama were talking."

Grandpa smiled from his mask of white. "Nothing moved along our street, but Miss Tims reported it. With her own twist on it, of course."

"Myrt Myers does that," said Kathleen. "Mama says she's a busybody."

Grandpa glanced away from the mirror he'd clamped to an open cupboard door. "I doubt if Miss Tims saw it that way. She *was* strong-minded, though, with peculiar prejudices. And forever giving advice."

"Mama doesn't like advice. Even Daddy says so."

"She always was an independent little mite," said Grandpa as Kathleen clamored up on the counter. He dipped his brush for more lather, adding, "I thought you and Charlie went riding."

63

"We did."

"Did Biscuit pitch him off up the street somewhere?"

"No. He's playing with Fawn Leroy. You should probably go get him."

"Oh? Why is that?"

"Because she made a face at me."

"She did? Now what do you suppose made her do that?"

"She's snippy." Kathleen paused as Grandpa pulled at his lip, making a smooth slope for his razor. "She has to be first at everything. Her mama makes her beautiful clothes and her uncle bought her a burro for the race. She doesn't even *like* burros."

"I declare," murmured Grandpa, razor clearing a path down one cheek.

Kathleen watched with growing impatience as the path widened stroke by stroke. "So are you going to go get him?"

"I reckon if the young lady is as unpleasant as you say, Charlie'll come home on his own."

"Fawn's pretending to be nice. She's a good actress. She fools the teacher sometimes."

"If you've got some free time, maybe you can spend a little of it with your grandpa."

"Okay," said Kathleen.

"First, let's have breakfast. Or have you eaten?"

Kathleen nodded. Grandpa reached for a towel and patted his face dry. "Then how'd you like to be my waitress?"

"Do you tip?"

Grandpa chuckled. "Depends on the service."

"It will be good service. The best service. Unless you order breakfast steak. That takes longer."

"Bacon and eggs will be fine." Grandpa put away his razor.

"Wait a minute, wait a minute! I'm not ready yet!"

Kathleen dashed upstairs and dressed for the part, pulling on one of Mama's old waitress uniforms. A pair of turquoise earrings added a nice grown-up touch. She painted on a little lipstick and sneezed as she powdered her nose.

Grandpa was waiting for her in the parlor. She took his hand. "Do you want to sit at the counter?"

"A table's fine. I like my eggs over easy," he added as they passed through to the restaurant.

"Wait, wait, wait! I have to write it down!"

Gram had already eaten. But Grandpa coaxed her into joining him for coffee. "Two coffees, one black, one cream," he said with a smile.

Kathleen scribbled across one of Mama's writing pads. "Now then, sir, do you want one egg or two?"

"Are they fresh?"

"Yes, sir."

"Make it two, then. And a slab of bacon. Does toast come with that?"

"Yes, sir."

"How about butter? Does butter come with the toast?"

Kathleen giggled. "Grandpa! You know it does!"

"I'd like some jelly, too. What kind do you have?"

"Grape, strawberry, cherry, and cactus jelly."

"Cactusberry?"

"No, cactus *jelly*. Daddy makes the best around."

"I'd better try some, then," said Grandpa.

Kathleen carried the ticket back to the serving window. She put silverware in her pocket, then took the coffee in two trips, careful not to slosh a drop. Captain Slade came in just as she was setting the second one down.

"Thought I'd stop by and pay off my debt before you sent a collector."

Kathleen ignored his friendly manner and asked, "Where's my cousin?"

"The baton twirler? He's leading my Sunshine all over the hillside on Patches. She's getting the hang of it." The Captain took a dollar from his pocket. "If you want to turn a profit on your money, bet it on those two in Saturday's race."

"I'm in the race, too," she said shortly.

"Oh. Good luck, then. You'll need it." Captain Slade tipped his fedora to Gram, nodded to Grandpa and turned away.

Kathleen stuffed the dollar in the pocket of her over-sized dress and took out the silverware. But all the fun had gone out of playing waitress. Gram slipped an arm around her waist.

"Why don't you sit down and have a glass of milk with us, darlin'?"

The restaurant door slammed before she could answer. It was Mrs. Leroy. Heads swiveled at the coffee cuppers' table as she confronted her brother.

"Batch, you get out there and you haul that animal out of my yard and don't you ever, ever pull such a stunt again!"

"That *animal* is a prize-winning burro. She's a shoo-in for Saturday's race," said the Captain.

"That wretched beast ate a pair of nylon stockings off my line and dragged a sheet through the dirt. If I hadn't gotten home when I did, she'd of eaten it, too!"

"I thought I tied her a safe distance . . ." the Captain began.

"The despicable creature chewed the rope through!" his sister cut him short.

"I'll replace your nylons and any other damage she's done."

"Forget the nylons. Just get that burro off my property!"

"Now, Gwen," soothed the Captain, fitting his hand to her elbow. "I've got friends coming in from out of town for Saturday's Jubilee. They're looking forward to seeing a good race."

"Gamblers, don't you mean?" Mrs. Leroy wrenched free, eyes glittering like quartz. "You've set this whole shindig up just for your own personal profit, haven't you, Batch?"

"That's not true." The Captain did his best to look injured. "The merchants'll make some money, outsiders'll see Oatman's still kicking, and everyone'll have a good time. Why, all Fawn needs is a little practice on that burro and she'll make us both proud. In the spirit of fun, of course."

"Spare me the song and dance, Batch. It's worry enough raising a child alone without living in the shadow of *your* reputation! I'm telling you one last time, you get out there and you get that burro off my property!" Mrs. Leroy stormed out the door.

Cactus Jack's was as silent as the sand in the bottom of the egg timer, every last patron watching through the window as the Captain hurried after his sister. Mrs. Leroy climbed in her car and slammed the door hard. The Captain leaned in the open window for a parting word, then jerked back as his sister pulled away, tires

67

spitting rocks all over his boots. Myrt Myers, who couldn't talk without whistling her "s" sounds, went off like a tea kettle at high boil.

"A shoo-in for Saturday's race, did you hear? Mister Slade's bringing in gamblers, the rascal! His sister's got his number, sure enough! He's pulled the wool over our eyes once again! Gambling on a race for kids! Has he no scruples?"

"Was that . . . ?" chimed Gram and Grandpa over the hiss of erupting tittle-tattle.

"Fawn's mama," said Kathleen.

Grandpa Dave slid back his chair. "I'll go get the boy. Kathleen, you want to tell me where the young lady lives?"

Mama came from the kitchen with Grandpa's plate. "Eat your breakfast, Dave. I'll get Charlie."

Kathleen lifted her skirt to accommodate a stride as long as her dress. "I'm coming, too!"

"No, Kathleen. Go change out of that dress, then help Gram run things until I get back."

Kathleen got over her disappointment between the restaurant and the parlor. *At least Charlie was coming back.* Fawn's loss, her gain. Not that she'd act over-eager. *No, sir. Charlie could just sweat it out while she gave him a dose of his own medicine.*

Kathleen froze in the act of ripping the dress over her head, for there on the red velvet sofa sat her Missouri cousin.

Eleven

———◆———

"Never mind, Mama. Charlie's back," Kathleen hollered into the restaurant. She discarded her dress, tucked her shirt into her pedal pushers, and raced back to the parlor to confront Charlie.

"Thought you were playing at Fawn's house."

Seeming not to notice her lofty sniff, Charlie said, "Fawn's mother started yelling when she saw Patches. She was going to chase her off with a clothesline prop, but Fawn stopped her."

"Why would Fawn stop her? She hates burros."

"Not Patches," said Charlie. "She cried and begged her mom to let her keep her for a pet."

"She didn't!"

"Sure enough," said Charlie. "But her mother said no, she wasn't about to be a party to the Captain's mischief. She said she was tired of people being so offish with her and Fawn on account of him."

"Offish?" echoed Kathleen.

"Unfriendly."

"What about Cookie?" huffed Kathleen. "*He's*

69

friendly with them. Friendlier than he is with me, and I've known him forever.''

Charlie shrugged. "All I know is Mrs. Leroy tore off in the car, saying she was going to set her brother straight once and for all."

"She *did* tell him off pretty good." At Charlie's questioning glance, Kathleen related what'd happened in the restaurant moments before.

"Sounds like she's still mad," said Charlie when Kathleen fell silent. He added, "Fawn asked me to bring Patches back to town where she'd be safe. Just in case the Captain didn't come after her, I mean."

"So where'd you leave her?"

Charlie jerked a thumb toward the back of the house. Kathleen tramped out the back door. Patches and Biscuit were locked neck over neck, grooming each other. Startled, she whirled on her cousin.

"She can't stay *here!*"

"I thought you liked Patches."

"I do. But Biscuit has to be in tip-top shape for the race. He can't be sharing food and a pen and making friends with the enemy!"

"Just because they're racing doesn't make them enemies," reasoned Charlie.

"Maybe not. But Fawn and I are!"

"Why?" asked Charlie.

Kathleen flung her arms wide. "I told you earlier. She always has to be first. And the best. And the prettiest and the smartest."

"Maybe you haven't given her a chance."

Kathleen narrowed her eyes. "What's *that* supposed to mean?"

Charlie tapped the sunbaked earth with the toe of his

70

shoe and wouldn't answer. The sun glinted off the pins on his chest, reminding her that he too took pride in honor bestowed. Kathleen thrust out her chin. "If you're thinking I'm jealous, you can just go soak your head!"

Charlie started across the yard without a word. He caught Patches's reins and led her to the gate.

"Are you taking her back?"

He shook his head no.

"Where, then?"

"I have to find another place where she'll be safe."

"Charlie!"

He led Patches out, then closed the gate and started away without looking back. Where was he taking her? And why was he being so stubborn about it? Patches wasn't *his* problem.

"Charlie!" Kathleen called again. "Just wait for Captain Slade. He'll come get her."

Charlie never even slowed down. Kathleen tore after him. "All right, all right! She can stay for now."

He turned back. "You mean it?"

"Until Captain Slade comes for her, anyway. It'll give me a chance to see how fast she can run." Kathleen saved face.

"Fawn isn't the only one who thinks she has to be first," muttered Charlie.

Kathleen dashed inside, pretending not to hear. Mama was refilling Gram and Grandpa's coffee cups. Quickly, she explained about Patches and got permission to ride down to the wash. The dried-up streambed outside of town was a perfect place for racing burros.

"Wait a second, you're forgetting something," Grandpa called after her. He reached into his pocket and pulled out a quarter. "Your tip for bringing my breakfast."

"Thanks, Grandpa." Kathleen pocketed the quarter and gave him a quick hug.

Charlie had mounted Biscuit in her absence, leaving Patches for Kathleen. They ambled out past the Tom Reed Mine and kept going until Oatman was well behind them. Old 66 was to their right, not a car in sight. Kathleen stopped to break a couple of switches off a paloverde tree. She passed one to Charlie, explaining that it took a bit of switching to keep a burro running.

"It's encouragement. It doesn't hurt them any more than a pat on the back hurts you or me," she assured.

Charlie nodded understanding.

Kathleen clamped her hat down tight. "Ready?" Seeing Charlie nod, she leaned low, hugged Patches with her knees and hollered, "On your mark. Get set. Go!"

They hit the dry wash at a run. Beside her, Biscuit moved in little bursts of speed with every touch of the switch. Patches, by contrast, ran at a quick steady pace. Half a mile down the wash, she was still fresh. But Biscuit was falling behind. Kathleen rode determinedly on, then glanced back again. Biscuit was starting to blow. He was trying his heart out, but he simply couldn't keep up. Abruptly, Kathleen stopped Patches and turned back, feeling heartsick. Biscuit was no match for the little jenny. If Fawn raced, she'd win for sure.

"Is there a prize for this race?" Charlie asked as they rested the burros.

Kathleen nodded. "Five dollars for first place. I could sure use the money. For the horse trailer, I mean."

Charlie scratched Biscuit's ears and said nothing.

72

"Biscuit can beat every other burro in the race." Slanting her cousin a glance, Kathleen added, "Guess all I can do is hope Fawn's mama won't let her race."

"Someone else might, though," said Charlie. "There must be other kids in town whose mothers wouldn't care."

Yet another problem! Kathleen groaned, for he was right. Captain Slade wasn't one to give up. Particularly if he had bets at stake. It was a pretty sure thing Patches would be in that race, with or without Fawn!

Old Coot was in Cactus Jack's when they returned. He often came in for a mid-morning coffee. But it was unusual to see Mama facing him across the table, sipping a cup, too. Hot and miserable and starting to tire, Kathleen wandered over and asked if Captain Slade had been there looking for Patches. Mama wagged her head.

"That young Jenny get away from Slade again?" asked Old Coot.

"Something like that," said Kathleen.

"Balky critter I could tell at a glance. Odds on you are lookin' better all the time." Old Coot stroked his whiskers, looking thoughtful. "May jest plump up my bet on that race."

Kathleen hoped he wouldn't. Maybe she had ought to warn him Biscuit's chances were pretty dim if Patches raced and to remind him what happened with his pickup truck. Course, likely as not he'd tell her to mind her manners and not talk back. She knocked a small spider off the wall and started to step on it when an idea so simple, so appealing, so absolutely perfect popped into her head that she spared the spider's life for providing the inspiration.

73

Kathleen slipped back through the parlor where the fan was whirring and on to the kitchen. Charlie came in just as she was taking Harriet's salad dressing jar out from under the sink.

"What're you doing?" he asked.

"Thinking," she said, hugging her secret close. "Just thinking."

Twelve

1. Bet everything on Biscuit.
2. Win the race.
3. Buy a used horse trailer with winnings.

The plan came to Kathleen full-blown. There were some bumps in it, though. For one thing, she knew nothing about betting. She couldn't ask Mama and Daddy. They were sure to forbid it. But Old Coot might help. Liking burros the way he did, he'd understand how desperate she was to save Biscuit.

Then there was Patches. If Captain Slade got someone other than Fawn to ride her, someone who wasn't afraid of spiders, her plan wouldn't work at all. It put her in the odd position of actually wanting "Has-To-Be-First" Fawn to be astride Patches on Saturday.

Too unsure of Charlie's loyalties to confide Harriet's part in her plan, Kathleen returned the tarantula to her home beneath the sink. "What do you want to do now?" she asked her cousin.

"Are you thirsty?" asked Charlie.

Kathleen nodded. Remembering her fun with Grandpa, she said, "Go sit at the counter and I'll be your waitress."

Mama had Kool-Aid made up in the refrigerator. Kathleen carried the pitcher out to the counter. But instead of spinning on the seat, Charlie was sitting perfectly still, staring out the wide front window. Kathleen felt the hair on her neck rise. Fawn Leroy! She was peeking through the glass, hands framing her face, baton clasped under one arm.

"Now what do you suppose *she* wants?"

Charlie's ears turned red.

"Charlie? May I come in?" Fawn called from the door.

Charlie jumped up so fast, he hit the Kool-Aid pitcher with his elbow. It splashed on his shirt, spread over the counter, and spilled onto the floor. He snatched a handful of napkins and sopped hastily at the mess. "Over here, Fawn." Voice dropping to a whisper, he pleaded, "Be nice to her, please?"

"Okay."

Charlie looked surprised. "You mean it?"

Thinking ahead to Saturday and knowing if her plan was to work, she'd have to get on better terms with Fawn, Kathleen shrugged. "I'll try."

Mama saw the mess and rushed over. "Go change your shirt, Charlie. I'll get a mop and clean this up."

But Fawn trapped Charlie before he could go. She glowed like a fiery sunset in her glittery baton-twirling dress and with her shining smile. "Mama's over being mad. She said it was real nice of you to take the burro away and that I could invite you to my house to play. Can you come, Charlie?"

Charlie's gaze crossed Kathleen's. He hesitated a second, then surprised Kathleen by asking, "Can Kathleen come, too?"

Fawn's hesitation was considerably longer. So long, it was insulting. But Kathleen struggled for the sake of her plan to be peaceable. "I can't right now. I've got something else to do."

Looking relieved, Fawn steadied her baton on the toe of her shoe. "Shall we go, Charlie?"

"I have to change my shirt," he said. "I'll be right back."

Kathleen could tell he wasn't sure she'd keep her word and be nice. Every few steps, he glanced back over his shoulder. Pretending not to notice, she stradled a counter stool and patted the one next to her. "You can sit down if you want."

Fawn eyed the stool narrowly and remained standing.

"Charlie says you've changed your mind about burros," Kathleen made another stab at honey over vinegar. "So?"

"I'm glad, that's all. I guess you'll be riding in the race now?"

"Maybe."

"Will you be taking Patches home with you? Now that your Mama's over being mad, I mean?" Kathleen tried one more time to nail down whether or not Fawn's mother was softening her position.

"Mama still doesn't like her," she admitted.

"Maybe she'll change her mind."

"Maybe," said Fawn, but she didn't sound too hopeful. She stretched out her baton as Charlie came rushing back.

"I'll be back in a little bit, okay?" Charlie said.

"Okay." Kathleen smiled sweet as pie. But on the inside she felt prickly as a cactus, watching her cousin and her enemy dash out the door together, each holding one end of the baton.

"You're free to go, too, Kathleen," said Mama as she came with the mop to clean around the base of the stool. "Run and catch up with them."

Kathleen sniffed. "What for? Fawn doesn't like me and I don't like her."

"You seemed to be getting along just now."

"I was being polite, that's all."

"Isn't there a chance, though, that you could be friends if you worked a little at understanding each other?" asked Mama.

Kathleen wrinkled her nose. "Fawn's too snippy and ruffly and curly."

"Charlie doesn't think so."

"He just met her. What's he know?"

"You know, Kathleen, when you judge a book by the cover, you never learn the story inside," said Mama. "That really isn't fair."

Kathleen frowned and lifted her head. "Are we still talking about Fawn?"

"This time, it's about Fawn. Next time, it'll be someone else. Maybe even us." Mama wrung out the mop, adding, "When we move, we'll be the new folks. I want people to know you by who you are, not by making a snap judgment concerning the way you look or dress or talk."

"Or who I'm related to?" said Kathleen, thinking of

78

Mrs. Leroy being sore over having to live down the Captain's reputation.

"You *do* understand!"

Only in part. But Mama sounded so pleased, she nodded. Old Coot was a distraction, stirring like he intended to leave. Remembering, Kathleen asked, "What were you and Old Coot talking about when I came in?"

Mama hesitated a moment, then said in a level voice, "He wanted to know the purchasing price of Cactus Jack's."

"Old Coot?" yelped Kathleen. "What would he want with a restaurant?"

"Shh!" warned Mama. Lowering her voice, she confided, "He wants to turn it into a bingo parlor."

"Jeepers!" It was like falling so hard, the air had whooshed out of her lungs. Watching the old prospector lay down his coffee money, Kathleen hopped down off her stool.

Mama caught her arm. "You aren't to question him, Kathleen. You know how touchy he is," she warned.

"I wasn't going to."

"I told you of his interest so you'd hear it from me rather 'n through Myrt Myers or some other busybody. That's what you wanted, isn't it?"

Kathleen nodded, feeling the weight of Mama's trust. She was still dreading the move and praying for a miracle to prevent it. But if one wasn't forthcoming, she'd rather Old Coot got the place than Captain Slade or someone she didn't know.

"I wanted to talk to him about the burro race, that's all. I won't mention the restaurant, honest Mama."

"See to it that you don't," said Mama.

Kathleen rushed out the door to overtake Old Coot,

questions fluttering in her head. "Mr. Coot, I was wondering . . . can I bet on myself? In the race, I mean?"

Old Coot stopped and swung around. His bushy brows drew together. "A sprout like you, betting? It ain't seemly."

Kathleen ignored an uncomfortable feeling inside and jutted out her lip. "You bet. So does Captain Slade. Why, he's got friends coming from out of town just to bet."

"On the race? You don't say!" Old Coot hooked his thumbs in his suspenders and limped along, brow furrowing furiously.

"He said so just a bit ago. Myrt Myers just about swallowed her hat when she heard."

"Confounded old meddler, I reckon she did." Coot tipped his ball cap to Miss Solomon who was coming down the walk toward them.

Preoccupied with her original question, Kathleen asked, "If I bet four dollars and sixty-five cents on myself, and I won, would I earn enough to buy a horse trailer?"

Overhearing, Solomon Sal stopped on the walk and looked back. "I wouldn't count on profiting from ill-gotten gain," she said.

Kathleen blurted, "But I need a horse trailer."

Solomon Sal looked from Kathleen to Old Coot. Her gaze narrowed. "Who planted the idea that a bet was the way to acquire it?"

Old Coot stuck out his jaw. "Now wait a dad-blamed minute. The little desert rat's asking questions, that's all."

"I wasn't accusing, only inquiring," said Solomon Sal.

"Then talk to the young 'un and leave me out of it!" Old Coot glowered at them both then stamped away.

Wishing just this once Miss Sal had kept her wisdom

to herself, Kathleen admitted, "He said it wasn't seemly. Betting, I mean."

"I'll apologize to him if I spoke out of turn." Miss Solomon squared her shoulders and resumed walking toward Cactus Jack's.

Beset by the helpless feeling that her plan was coming apart, Kathleen started after her. "Miss Solomon? How much do you think a horse trailer would cost?"

Miss Solomon stroked her sun-baked nose. "Does this have to do with Biscuit and your move to Illinois?"

Kathleen nodded and told her the sum total of her savings. "How much more would I need?"

"There was a used one advertised in the *Mohave Miner* for fifty dollars."

"Fifty dollars! How am I going to get that kind of money?"

Miss Solomon caught Kathleen's hands in her own and turned her palms up. "The same way you got these blisters. Work for it."

Work for it. Making sure Fawn was the rider aboard Patches on race day was going to be work, suspicious as she was of Kathleen's changed manner. Figuring out how to bet—that'd be work, too. And finding a way to slip Harriet close enough to Fawn to scare her right off Patches's back at the most crucial moment of the race was going to be the hardest work of all.

Yessir, she sure enough had her work cut out. It bothered her some, knowing Miss Solomon and Old Coot wouldn't be the only ones disappointed in her methods. But with Biscuit's future at stake and time growing short, she'd just have to risk getting her halo a bit tarnished.

Thirteen

———◆———

Kathleen sat down with last Thursday's copy of the weekly *Mohave Miner* and searched until she found the advertisement about the horse trailer. A little more thinking made her realize she had gotten ahead of herself. Best find out for sure that a lack of transportation was all that was keeping Mama and Daddy from agreeing to take Biscuit along. If she was facing opposition beyond that, she needed to know before she went out of her way being nice to Fawn. Not to mention dabbling in gambling.

With that in mind, Kathleen took the newspaper into the restaurant kitchen where Mama was stirring a creamy dressing into potato salad-makings. Kathleen read the advertisement to her.

"Moving all that way is expensive. We're going to have to be awful close with our money," cautioned Mama.

"I'll earn the money myself."

"That's a lot of nickels and dimes."

"I know. But if I find a way to earn it, we can take Biscuit with us, can't we?"

"There are other things to consider." Mama sliced hard-boiled eggs on top of the salad. "That paper's five days old. The trailer may have sold already."

"But if it isn't sold, and I do earn the money, can we take Biscuit with us?"

Mama bumped into her, reaching for the waxed paper. She moved her hands like she was shooing flies. "Ask your father, Rose Kathleen. I'm busy with lunch."

Daddy'd taken Grandpa and Gram Sophie up to Elephant Tooth Rock. Kathleen sat in the shade of the front awning, shuffling concerns as she awaited their return. She'd landed on Old Coot's bad side without learning a thing about betting. She hadn't any guarantee Fawn would be the one riding Patches in Saturday's race. And what if she went to all this trouble, and Mama and Daddy still wouldn't take Biscuit along? Itchy over "what ifs," Kathleen closed her eyes and promised God she'd be good as could be from now on if He'd just make it so she wouldn't have to give up her pet as well as her home.

Hearing footsteps, she opened her eyes. Captain Slade was strolling down the walk toward her, peeling the wrapper off a cigar.

"Your burro's out back," she called to him.

He clamped the cigar between his teeth and struck a wooden match with his thumbnail. "I saw you racing her earlier this morning. You ride pretty well for a girl."

"I could teach Fawn to ride just as good."

"So she can race? Now that's real sporting of you. Particularly when you're competing for that first prize money yourself."

Kathleen overlooked his dry tone and said bluntly, "If I was to teach her, I'd want a favor in return."

83

"Oh? And what would that be?"

"I'd want you to place a bet on the race for me."

The Captain's wary look gave way to amusement. He shook out the match and tossed it into the street. "That so?"

"And you'd have to keep it a secret," she added. "Mama'd be mad if she knew."

"Can't say I'm surprised."

"So do we have a deal?" asked Kathleen.

He drew a long hard pull on his cigar. "How big of a bet are we talking about?"

"Four dollars and sixty-five cents. That's all the money I have. Unless you want to loan me five," Kathleen pushed boldly ahead. "Which is what I'll make when I win first prize. Then I'll pay you back."

"Cheeky, aren't you?"

"I know which burro's going to win, that's all."

"So if I were to loan you five, you'd be placing a nine dollar and sixty-five cent bet?" The Captain's smile bore a striking resemblance to a coyote grin.

"Is that enough to win fifty dollars?"

"That depends on the odds and whether you've picked the winning burro. Then there's the matter of my commission."

"Commission?" she echoed.

"Interest on the five I'd be loaning you."

Was he teasing? Or was he trying to cheat her? Kathleen balled sweaty hands into hard fists and poked out her chin. "Never mind loaning me five, then. Just bet my four dollars and sixty-five cents."

"On Patches?" he asked.

"No! On my burro, Biscuit."

Captain Slade tossed back his head and laughed.

"Girlie, you might just as well toss your money down a hole, all the good it'll do you on a wager like that."

"I won't lose," Kathleen retorted. "I can't. I have to buy a horse trailer with my winnings so when we move I can take Biscuit with me."

"If that old-timer of yours beats Patches, I'll *give* you a trailer!" he declared.

Kathleen treated it like a serious offer, repeating it back. "I help Fawn get ready to race, I beat her, and you'll get me a trailer?"

The Captain's boastful laugh faded. He scanned the paper she shoved in his face, then passed it back, saying, "Tell you what, missy. You keep Patches here where Fawn can come practice and you'll get your trailer."

Kathleen asked, "What about Fawn's mama?"

"She doesn't have to know. Just invite Sunshine over to play and ride where Gwen won't see you . . . and win the race."

"What if Myrt Myers catches wind of it? Or somebody else tells?" asked Kathleen.

"We'll cross that bridge when we come to it. So do we have an agreement?"

Kathleen shook the hand he extended. "We do now."

"Good luck to you then. It's been a pleasure." The Captain tipped his hat and walked on.

Kathleen picked at a jagged thumbnail, pretty well pleased with the deal. There was no betting involved, which relieved her conscience considerably. All she had to do now was board Patches, teach Fawn to ride, and win the race. How hard could *that* be?

Fourteen

⊷◆⊶

Kathleen told Daddy, as soon as he returned from Elephant Tooth Rock, that the Captain would buy her a horse trailer in return for board for Patches and riding lessons for Fawn. She didn't mention that Biscuit had to win Saturday's race for the deal to be valid. Or that the Captain had originally made the offer in jest, poking fun at her confidence in Biscuit.

"You should have held out for cash up front," said Daddy dryly.

Quickly, she replied, "The Captain'll come through. We shook on it."

Daddy read the ad in lieu of a response. When pressed, he agreed that if the trailer materialized, he'd think about taking Biscuit to Illinois with them.

That was almost as good as a "yes." *Finally, real progress!* Eager to proceed with her part of the deal, it seemed too coincidental to Kathleen when Charlie returned with Fawn in tow.

Fawn squared her shoulders and said right off, "Wesley gave me money to eat lunch here. He and Mama have gone into Kingman to shop.''

"Tenderloin is today's special," Kathleen ignored the snip in Fawn's voice. "It comes with red beans and potato salad."

Fawn ordered a hamburger instead. But Charlie had a tenderloin and so did Kathleen. They sat at the counter and twirled on their seats while Mama cooked and Gram brought Delaware Punch and silverware.

Kathleen was afraid to tell Fawn the deal she'd made with Captain Slade for fear she'd out and out refuse to cooperate. Smarter to coax her into riding without any mention of "teaching." And what better bait than Charlie?

She licked ketchup from her fingers and asked, "Want to go see my favorite tailing pond when we're done eating, Charlie?"

"Can Fawn come, too?"

"If she wants to. We can take some empty Log Cabin syrup tins and set them up like a village."

"How about it, Fawn?" asked Charlie.

Fawn frowned and hesitated a moment. But finally she said, "I guess so. Just so long as Mama doesn't find out."

Kathleen wasn't surprised to hear that the tailing ponds worried Mrs. Leroy. They were left from the days when the mines were operating and cyanide was used to extract gold from the ore. "Just keep your hands away from your face. That's what Mama says."

"And you can practice your riding on the way," Charlie added.

It was almost as if he'd read Kathleen's mind! Or was it? Seeing a whisper pass between them, Kathleen wrestled jealousy's sharp prick and made the most of the opening. "You'd better practice all you can if you're going to be in Saturday's race."

Fawn neither admitted nor denied such intentions.

Kathleen finished eating first. She tossed her tin cabins into a paper bag and had the burros all ready by the time Charlie and Fawn came out back. She mounted up and stretched a hand down to Charlie, saying, "How about carrying the sack of tins?"

Charlie opened the gate first, then settled behind Kathleen, and took the paper bag. Patches bolted out of the yard, demanding her own head.

"Rein her in," Kathleen hollered as the little jenny bounced Fawn about.

"I'm trying!"

"Use your hands and a stern voice. Hug with your knees."

"I kn-o-o-o-w!"

"Don't be afraid to switch her, she's got to know who's boss," Kathleen hollered.

"Uncle . . . Batch . . . said . . . that . . . too." Fawn's voice quivered like she was shouting through a fan.

"Left. Make her go left. Out toward the Tom Reed. Pull on the rein. That's it. Watch out for the jumping cactus!"

It was a rough start. But once Fawn got control of Patches, she did a fair job of following the directions Kathleen called to her. Was it the same competitive drive that pushed her to the head of the class in music and spelling and geography and story writing that had helped her conquer her fear? Giving Fawn grudging marks for grit, Kathleen prodded Biscuit into the lead and kept it the rest of the way.

88

Years ago, when the Tom Reed Mine was still in operation, the ore was crushed then agitated in cyanide tanks as part of the gold-extracting process. The residue from the agitation tank, or tailings, as it was called, was piped out and poured down the hillside where it settled and dried into a hard pinkish white heap. Years and years of such dumping had left a pile of "tailings" bigger than a baseball field and twenty-foot high at its peak. Spring rains filled the washes that ran down the mountainside and had, over time, carved perpendicular trails through the tailing piles.

"Watch out for the creosote bushes," Kathleen warned Charlie. She pointed out the green shrubs as Biscuit picked his way up the pile of tailings. "It's sticky and it'll get on your clothes and it stinks."

She dumped the sack of empty tins and divvied them up. She and Fawn combined their tins to make a small pioneer village. Charlie settled nearby and made a fort with his cluster of tins.

"I know!" said Fawn. "Let's gather some sticks and make little tepees out of this sack."

"An Indian village. Good idea!" said Charlie.

Kathleen scrambled down the pile and gathered some tiny stones. She made a fire pit inside the tepee she fashioned then shredded some creosote leaves.

"I thought you said not to touch those," said Fawn.

"You can if you're making creosote tea," Kathleen amended, as she stirred her leaves with a stick.

"Tea? *Phew,* it stinks!" Fawn challenged.

"I know. But my grandmother has a bellyache. The medicine man said give her creosote tea."

"Maybe she has the measles like my sister," Fawn played along. "She caught them from the white trader."

89

"Measles?" Charlie slid down the tailing pile to join them. "I'll be the new chief. See, the old chief died. He had the measles, too." He scratched his spiky hair and added, "Lots and lots of my people are sick. It's the chief's job to get even."

"What're you going to do?" asked Fawn.

Charlie screwed his mouth to one side. "Attack the pioneer village."

Kathleen watched as he slipped quietly up the tailing pile and took a stick girl hostage. "She wouldn't go that easy," she pointed out. "She'd fight!"

Charlie dropped the stick girl and dusted his hands. "I know! Let's use the burros and act it out."

Fawn scrambled to her feet beside him. "I'll be the kidnapped girl."

"Biscuit'll be my pony. Pretend I captured him on the desert and tamed him myself," said Charlie. He smeared two streaks of desert dust on his sweaty face, then stripped to the waist and swung up on Biscuit.

"You can be Fawn's sister," he called to Kathleen. Then he leaned down to haul Fawn up behind him, adding, "Run to the fort to get help."

Forgetting her own words about putting up a fight, Fawn looked pretty eager for a girl being kidnapped. "Run fast. I'm your *only* sister! My life is in mortal danger! Scream and cry and pull your hair."

Kathleen's fingers itched to pull hair, sure enough. But she let out a blood-curdling scream instead. Biscuit wheeled around in alarm. Fawn lost her grip and fell off. She jumped up and dusted herself off, calling, "Try it again, Charlie."

Charlie's second pass was meant to be even more dramatic. This time *he* toppled off Biscuit's back trying

90

to pull Fawn up behind him without stopping. Biscuit stopped and waited patiently for him to mount again.

Each time they enacted the scene, Fawn got to be the fair maiden in distress while Kathleen had to play her hysterical sister. Finally Charlie changed roles and plotted a rescue, casting himself as lieutenant of the cavalry.

"It's Kathleen's turn," said Fawn, dusting herself off. "I'll be the Indian brave standing guard and you can pretend to slip in and steal her away, okay?"

Kathleen hid her surprise and sniffed. "I wouldn't need rescuing, I'd get away on my own."

"I know!" cried Fawn. "Let's play a new game. We're Amazon women like we studied in school. Our home is deep in the forest. We'll drag Charlie there and make him our servant."

"I wouldn't live in a forest even if I *was* an Amazon," said Kathleen.

"You'd have to if you were an Amazon," said Charlie.

"Would not. I'd be a *desert* Amazon. They're ten times tougher than forest Amazons." Kathleen dove at him just to prove it.

Fawn giggled and lunged at him, too.

Charlie slumped to the ground with a theatrical flare.

"Soperab neg leo?" Fawn rattled off strange words.

"Do you give up?" Kathleen pretended to translate.

Charlie cracked one eye and whispered, "I would, but I'm out cold."

Kathleen couldn't stay cross, he was such a good sport. Fawn helped her blindfold him with his shirt, saying, "He mustn't see the way to our forest home."

"Desert home," corrected Kathleen.

"That either," said Fawn. She mounted Patches and

scouted ahead. She made up swamps to cross and poisonous snakes hanging from pretend trees and cannibals chasing them across a waterless desert. It was such a dangerous journey; the captured servant became a trusted friend in their struggle to survive.

It was the most fun Kathleen'd had since Binky'd moved away. They used Charlie's shirt for collecting the Log Cabin tins since they'd cut up the paper sack. On the ride home, Kathleen told Fawn that Captain Slade had arranged to leave Patches at her house until after the race.

"You don't mind?" asked Fawn.

Kathleen shrugged and said, "I like Patches."

Fawn cocked her head to one side and asked straight out, "How come you're being nice?"

"You changed your mind about burros, didn't you?" said Kathleen.

"You changed your mind about me because I changed my mind about burros?"

Kathleen crossed her fingers behind her back. "Something like that."

Fawn's smile lost its wariness. "I'm glad."

Feeling a twinge of conscience, Kathleen was silent as they rode on. At the outskirts of town, Fawn dismounted and turned Patches over to Charlie. "I'd better walk from here."

Knowing Fawn didn't want her mother to catch her riding, Kathleen said, "You can come after school tomorrow, if you want."

"And play again? You mean it?"

Kathleen nodded as Charlie mounted Patches.

"I'd like that." Smiling, Fawn started away, then turned back to wave. "Thanks for the nice time," she called. "I'll see you tomorrow, Charlie. You too, Kathleen."

Kathleen felt a second jab over her ulterior motives. But she lifted her hand, reasoning that Biscuit's future depended upon her plan. Fawn had to ride in the race. And Biscuit had to win. It was that simple.

Fifteen

Kathleen was leaving for school the next morning when she saw Fawn peeking in the front window of Cactus Jack's. She dashed out the back way, skipped her hand over Biscuit's back as she flew past and sneaked around to the front.

"If you're looking for Charlie, he isn't up yet."

Fawn jumped back from the glass so quick, she dropped her baton. "He isn't coming to school?"

Kathleen wagged her head. "His teacher sent his assignments along, but he's got plenty of time to do them. They aren't starting home until after the race on Saturday."

"So soon?"

Kathleen nodded. Face falling, Fawn picked up her baton and gave it a twirl. She pitched the thing into the air and caught it without hitting herself in the nose or the eyes, then stopped and looked both ways before crossing Main Street. "Charlie said this highway goes all the way to his home in Missouri and right past his front door."

"I know. He counted license plates from seventeen different states. He's going to turn the list into his teacher as an extra credit report."

"I guess it isn't 66 anymore," Fawn corrected herself. She paused in the middle of the road. "Now that the new road's open, I mean. Have you ridden on it?"

Kathleen shook her head no. "Have you?"

"Yes. Wesley took us the day the road opened. We got on the new highway in Topock and followed it back to Kingman," said Fawn. "It was fun, being one of the first."

Kathleen thought of Binky and how they'd spied on Fawn and her mama and Wesley that day and wondered where they were going. Though it'd been only a month, all the changes made it seem like a long time ago. Businesses folding. Folks moving. How long before they moved, too? Soon, maybe, if Old Coot bought Cactus Jack's. Her stomach lurched.

"Is it still okay if I come to your house after school?" Fawn cut into her thoughts.

Kathleen nodded. "We'll go riding."

"I'd like that." Fawn smiled, and a short time later, when it came time for oral reading, she actually put her hand down. With Kathleen's the only hand left waving, the teacher called on her first.

Kathleen's surprise gave way to caution in the face of such uncharacteristic behavior. She reminded herself that Fawn wanted to come to her house because of Charlie. Just like she wanted Fawn to be in the race because of Biscuit. It wasn't friendship, for friendship wouldn't make you feel like you'd sneaked a look off someone else's test paper.

Lunchtime seemed forever in coming. Kathleen raced

home to eat and found Charlie sitting in front of the fan with his shirt off. "Fawn's coming right after school to go riding," she told him.

"Riding? I should say not!" Gram Sophie marched into the parlor with a dishpan of water.

"Please, Gram? I'll be better by then," pleaded Charlie.

"Certainly not. You'll be lucky if you don't blister!"

Belatedly, Kathleen saw that his back and his arms and his chest were as red as raw meat. "Jeepers! How'd you get so burned?"

"Running around shirtless, that's how." Gram dipped a dish towel in the pan of water. Charlie winced at the touch of the cold towel against his skin. "Easy," said Gram. "This should draw out the heat."

Kathleen's skin felt warm just looking at him. "Solomon Sal put animal salve on my friend Binky when he caught his pants on fire. He said it helped a heap."

"A cool rag is good enough. Thanks, Gram," said Charlie.

"You sit right here now and do your homework. You aren't to even think of going outdoors, you hear me?" Gram warned one last time as she started away.

"You and Fawn will have to go without me," said Charlie when Gram had gone back to the kitchen.

"We could play inside instead," Kathleen made a token offer.

"No! Fawn needs the practice if she's going to ..." Charlie stopped short.

"Going to *what?*"

Charlie dropped his gaze to his science book.

"Be in Saturday's race? Is that what you two were whispering about yesterday?" Kathleen prodded.

Charlie's sigh was confession enough. Marking his place with his finger, he said, "Help her, Kathleen. Please?"

"Why should I?"

"So she can have fun."

"She always has fun. She wins everything at school. Just ask her."

Carefully, Charlie peeled the rag off his shoulder, dipped it in the water and said no more. Nor did Kathleen admit she was already committed to helping Fawn for reasons all her own.

Fawn came after school as planned, bringing her baton along with her. Her riding was pretty fair and her twirling improved too after an indoor lesson from Charlie. She worked hard, took criticism well, and thanked Kathleen for her trouble. But Kathleen held herself off from having fun the way they'd done yesterday at the tailing pond. With Biscuit's future hanging on Saturday's race, it was best to keep in mind the little snip who'd beaten her out of every honor at school, then twisted about in her fussy dresses, just rubbing it in.

Following her lead, Fawn observed what could best be termed an unspoken truce. No snubs. No poked-out tongues. But no giggles or shared secrets either. Her riding showed more confidence on Wednesday and Thursday. So much so, Kathleen took extra care with Harriet, making sure she stayed in good health.

By Friday, Charlie was shedding worse than Biscuit in the springtime. He begged to go with Kathleen and Fawn as they prepared to ride out, but Gram blocked the door, claiming he'd burn over his burn, and Maggie'd never trust her again, having let him get in such a shape.

Kathleen nudged Biscuit into the lead and didn't stop until they'd reached a remote spot beyond the eyes of the town. She gestured toward a jagged pile of boulders way off on the horizon.

"There's a boarded-up mine shaft about a half a mile from here. On the count of three, we're going to race to it. Pretend it's the real thing."

"All out?" asked Fawn.

"All out."

Kathleen gathered the reins in her fingers, hunched forward and gave the count. Biscuit stretched out his neck at the touch of the switch and broke away to lead. But it didn't take Patches long to catch up. The burros stayed even the first quarter-mile. Then Patches started inching away. Inches became feet until Kathleen and Biscuit were plunging through dust raised by Patches's pounding hooves. Kathleen reined Biscuit in short of the appointed finish line, slipped off his back, and patted his heaving chest.

"Don't worry about it, Biscuit. We aren't licked yet," she whispered.

Fawn turned back, too. Kathleen braced herself for the expected, "I won!" But it never came. They walked the burros home, letting them cool down.

Charlie came out the back door as they closed the burros in. His shirt hid his scaling chest and back, but his peeling nose was stuck right out there, curious to know what'd caused the strained silence.

"Are you ready for the race tomorrow?" he asked in a general way that included both of them.

Kathleen nodded. But Fawn just kept brushing Patches.

"What's the matter? Are you worried about your mama finding out?" he asked finally.

Fawn shook her head. "Wesley's going to keep her down by the finish line. By the time Mama figures it out, it'll be too late."

Startled, Kathleen swung around. "You mean Wesley knows you're racing?"

Fawn nodded. "Uncle Batch told him. He was hoping he'd help."

"And Cookie didn't tell your mama? Why not?" asked Kathleen.

"He knows she wouldn't let me race if she knew."

"Because your uncle made bets?"

"That's what Mama says. But really, she's just scared I'll get hurt." Frustration spilled over Fawn's words.

"And Cookie's taking *your* side?"

"No," Fawn said sharply. "Taking my side would be telling Mama she's wrong. He's not going to do that."

Knowing Cookie, he was too short on words for such a conversation. Kathleen chewed her lip, glad she didn't have to sneak around Mama just to have fun. She stopped short at the thought. Was that what Charlie'd been trying to tell her before? That Mrs. Leroy's worries got in the way sometimes? Catching Charlie looking at her, she poked out her chin and said, "Better not let Gram catch you out here."

Charlie grinned at her for no reason at all. "Sun or no sun, Gram's not stopping me tomorrow. I'm going to the race and cheering for you both."

Kathleen and Fawn traded wary glances. Seeming not to notice, Charlie unfastened two of his perfect atten-

99

dance pins. He gave one to Kathleen and one to Fawn, keeping the remaining one on his shirt. "These are for luck," he said. "And for friendship."

Fawn pinned hers on her starched collar. But Kathleen hesitated.

"Put it on," urged Charlie. "And agree to go on being friends, no matter who wins."

"That's nice, Charlie." Fawn smiled tentatively and held out her hand.

Kathleen hesitated a long moment before shaking on it. She even managed to smile. But not without thinking of Harriet and feeling false as the Captain's front teeth.

Sixteen

※

Daddy wanted everything shipshape for the next day's festivities. Once they'd closed for the evening, he sent Kathleen and Charlie out front to sweep the boardwalk. They swept by the light of the street lamp then balanced the broom over the hitching post and took turns trying to catapult each other into the air. Kathleen was on the "send-off" end when the handle snapped. She went sprawling on her backside.

"Oops! Are you all right?" asked Charlie.

"Course." Catching a glimpse of Daddy wagging his head on the other side of the window, Kathleen jumped up real quick and shouted so he'd hear through the glass, "Sorry about the broom, Daddy."

Down the walk, a familiar voice hollered, "Best stick to burros, young 'un. Them broomsticks'll buck you off every time." It was Old Coot limping toward her.

Pleased he was over being miffed, Kathleen greeted the bewhiskered old prospector with a smile. " 'Evening, Mr. Coot."

"Are ya ready for tomorrow's race?"

"Ready to win," she said.

"You better, or I'll come after ya with the other end of that broom!"

Kathleen grinned. "Yessir."

Old Coot spat toward the street and shifted a cigar box under his arm. "Yer folks around?"

"They're tidying up inside for the Jubilee tomorrow. Should bring us some extra business."

"Dad-blamed nonsense," groused Old Coot as he angled for the door.

The moment he'd gone in, Kathleen and Charlie pressed their faces to the glass, curious to see what was in the cigar box. Old Coot sat down near the window and waited for Mama and Daddy to come over before opening the lid. Kathleen caught a flash of green before Mama jumped up and let the blinds down. Her heart plummeted.

"What's he doing?" asked Charlie.

Buying the place. That's what Old Coot was doing. Even though she'd been preparing herself for just such an event, Kathleen couldn't fight back the tears. She tore up the street alone and didn't stop running until she'd reached Solomon Sal's front porch.

Miss Solomon was taking her ease on the paint-bare bench just like she did every night. "Nice breeze, isn't it?" she called.

"Old Coot's buying the place," Kathleen blurted. She tried to swallow the painful lump in her throat. "We'll have to move to my uncle's now for sure."

"You must be feeling pretty rough, then." Solomon Sal's voice was soft with sympathy. She patted the bench, an invitation for Kathleen to come join her.

But Kathleen was too jumpy to sit. Out on the desert,

a coyote called. The lonesomeness of it brought fresh tears. She stamped across the porch boards, muttering, "Illinois is a rotten place."

"I didn't realize you'd been there."

"I haven't. But I hate it anyway."

Miss Solomon got to her feet. She wandered to the end of the porch and lifted her face to the sky, saying in rich quiet tones, " 'The sun has one kind of splendor, the moon another and the stars another; and star differs from star in splendor.' "

The words were too big to enclose in a mind so anxious. Kathleen kicked an old tin cup and sent it clattering across the porch.

"That's from Isaiah." Miss Solomon's hands settled on Kathleen's stiff shoulders. "It's true about all the earth under the sky, too. Whether it's a city or a town or a mountain or a valley or a little maple camp somewhere, each place has its own splendor."

"I won't like it. I know I won't," said Kathleen.

"Not if you take that attitude, no. Better to keep your thoughts open as the Milky Way." Miss Solomon lifted an arm and pointed, saying, "See there, how it's splashed across the sky?"

Kathleen couldn't resist a gander at the star-dimpled heavens. Nowhere else in the world could the sky be so beautiful. It was so close, the stars seemed to skip over the moutaintops.

"See the Big Dipper?" said Miss Solomon. "And Pleiades?"

A marvel for sure—though you probably couldn't see the constellations in Dry Grove. Not with those big trees Mama loved choking up the sky.

"You're tough like these mountains," said Miss Solomon after a bit. "You'll transplant just fine. And when you're all grown up if this special piece of country's still calling you, why you'll find your way back."

It was small comfort. But comfort all the same. Kathleen slipped a hand into Solomon Sal's and stood a long time, memorizing the sky.

When she finally walked home, Cactus Jack's was dark. But there was a light burning over the parlor table where Mama was filling out papers. Gram and Grandpa were stirring upstairs, Charlie was out back with the burros, and Daddy had gone for a walk. Nocturnal, thought Kathleen. Like Harriet.

Slipping into the parlor, she said, "Old Coot bought us, didn't he Mama?"

Mama lifted her head from her papers. "He bought Cactus Jack's, darlin'. He didn't buy us."

Somehow, it felt like he had, it was that hard to separate herself from her home.

She swallowed the lump in her throat and asked, "How soon are we leaving for Illinois?"

"Soon," said Mama. "Soon."

Kathleen had trouble falling asleep. She overslept the next morning, dressed in a rush, and hurried downstairs to find the kitchen empty. Gram, Grandpa, and Daddy were all helping Mama in the restaurant. Kathleen saw at a glance that business was brisk. Most of the faces were unfamiliar. It wasn't yet eight o'clock, and already the Jubilee was drawing a crowd. Charlie was out back, feeding the chickens.

Too nervous for breakfast, Kathleen went out too, and began grooming Biscuit. Charlie offered to help, but it was something she wanted to do alone. Seeming to understand, he fed Patches a carrot before going inside, leaving Kathleen alone with her pet. By nine o'clock, Biscuit's coat was shining. His hooves gleamed brighter than Buster Brown's shoes and his teeth looked like a Pepsodent billboard.

Kathleen hugged his neck and crooned, "Don't you look fine! Such a sweet, pretty baby. Gonna win the race today, aren't you? Gonna show Fawn and Captain Slade and all the rest just what a tough old fella you are!"

Charlie circled around from the front walk with Fawn on his heels. She was dressed in white from the ribbon in her hair to her eyelet shirt and blousy shorts right down to her lacey anklets. She must have polished the pin Charlie gave her, for it gleamed from her collar like a shiny new coin. "They're about to start the coaster races," Charlie said. "Are you coming?"

Kathleen wagged her head no. "The race is in an hour. I've gotta polish my boots."

"You better come, Kathleen. Binky's down at the finish line looking for you."

Kathleen swung around. "Binky's here?"

Fawn nodded. "His brothers brought him so he could see you race."

"Are you coming?" Charlie asked again.

"You two go ahead. I'll catch up later."

Kathleen heard the starter gun fire. She heard the creak, rattle and rumble of homemade coaster cars rolling down Main Street accompanied by the cheers of an enthusiastic crowd. But she couldn't go. Not even to see Binky. The burro race followed the coasters, and she had to be ready.

It was quiet in the kitchen as Kathleen took Harriet's

jar from beneath the sink and set it on the table. Her brown vest was hanging over a chair, Charlie's gift pin tacked to it. It was an old vest, but Gram had dressed it up with some fringe. She had added, at Kathleen's request, a nice big pocket to the left of the row of buttons. The needle, the thread and the pin cushion were still on the table.

Kathleen threaded the needle, tied a knot in the end of the thread and slowly unscrewed the lid from the jar. She opened the pocket, angled the jar, and gently shook Harriet inside. It was a good fit and nocturnal Harriet, liking the dark folds, made no attempt to crawl out. Carefully, Kathleen sewed the pocket closed. Her stitches were long and uneven, but they'd keep Harriet from escaping, should the noise of the crowd frighten her. Kathleen left one end of the thread unknotted so when the time was right, she could pull the stitches out with a single tug. She returned the pins to the pin cushion and put the empty jar beneath the sink.

It'd taken longer than she'd thought. She heard Charlie and Fawn return. Charlie's voice rang through the quiet kitchen as he opened the back door. "Kathleen? Are you ready? The coast races are over."

"I'm coming!" Nerves tightening, Kathleen skipped a rag over her boots, donned her hat and slipped on the vest. But at the door, she turned back. Her fingers were clumsy with hurrying as she unfastened Charlie's pin and dropped it on the table.

This wasn't about friendship. This was about winning.

Seventeen

Give the Captain his dues—the Jubilee had drawn a terrific crowd. All those strangers waiting for the race to begin gave Kathleen the jitters. She rode Biscuit down the street toward the bend in the road where eight kids and eight burros waited behind the barricades. Captain Slade was there too, showing his new teeth in a coyote smile as his out-of-town friends thumbed through their wallets.

"Don't let her size fool you, this lady can ride," Kathleen heard him say as she approached. "Her burro has a nice even temperament, too."

"Little long in the tooth, isn't he?" asked a fellow with a patch over one eye.

Kathleen frowned at the Captain's friend. "Biscuit's ten, the same as me."

"Prime of life for a burro," claimed the Captain.

A short, bowlegged man pointed out a husky burro that Biscuit had beaten not more than a week ago. "How about that feller? He's purty muscular."

"A good strong runner," said the Captain.

"I'm putting my money on this old boy right here," a big red-haired fella threw his support behind Biscuit.

"Excellent choice! I'd bet on him myself if it wasn't for Sunshine." The Captain lowered his voice and glanced surreptitiously at his niece. "Can't very well bet against her. Like I said, this is her first race."

The man scratched his red head and winked at his pals. "I declare, that *is* Sunshine, big as life. First I've seen of her since she moved up here. When'd Gwen let her out of the play pen?"

The man with the wishbone legs took a gander at Fawn and joined the ribbing. "Growing up fast, ain't she? Gwen better get ready to loosen up those apron strings."

"Loosen? She'll strangle Batch with 'em if she catches her baby on that burro!" said the one-eyed man.

The men traded sly grins, elbows nudging the neighboring ribs.

Taking their gang-up in stride, the Captain said without a hint of injury, "Gwen means well. She's had a rough time since Fawn's daddy was killed, that's all."

Looking faintly ashamed, his friends quit their teasing and got down to the business of betting. Kathleen could tell they weren't aware of Patches's past success in racing. The Captain wasn't going to tell them, that's for sure. His every word and gesture was aimed at dismissing Fawn as a real contender. Winning bets was his main concern. Glad that the Captain wasn't *her* uncle, Kathleen watched his friends amble down the street toward the finish line and wished he'd disappear with them.

"Move back, folks, before someone gets kicked. We're going to get these burros lined up. Find a spot along the route," said the fire chief, who was in charge of the race.

As the people began moving away, Kathleen's old pal Binky came bursting through the barricades. He cocked his gap-toothed grin and challenged, "Hey! What'd I tell you? A shot at winning was just too good to resist for Miss Smarty Pants."

Knowing he meant Fawn, Kathleen shushed him and conceded in a whisper, "You and Richie were right. The Captain bought her a burro. How's Kingman?" she asked in a louder voice, just so Fawn wouldn't think they were talking about her should she happen to overhear.

"Fine." Striding closer, Binky shot a look over his shoulder at Fawn and back again. "You could get lucky if the race is delayed much longer," he whispered behind his hand.

"Lucky? How do you mean?"

"Fawn's mother is on her way to stop Miss Priss."

Kathleen blinked in alarm. "She knows Fawn's racing?"

"I heard Myrt Myers telling her just a minute ago."

"That old busybody!" cried Kathleen.

Puzzled, Binky said, "I thought you'd be glad. You want her out of the race, don't you?"

Kathleen flushed, ill-prepared to explain her sudden sympathy for Fawn. She hardly understood it herself as Mrs. Leroy elbowed through the crowd like Moses parting the Red Sea. The Captain's sister stopped short at the sight of Fawn aboard Patches. Her mouth thinned, her eyes flashed.

"Fawn Leroy, shame on you! Sneaking behind my back! Get off that creature right now!" Mrs. Leroy whirled around and gave her brother a dose of wrath too. "You just couldn't take no for an answer could you, Batch? You're worse than a seven-year plague!"

"Now, Gwen," the Captain began.

"It isn't Uncle's fault," Fawn interrupted. "I begged him not to tell you because I knew you'd be scared. Can't I race, Mama? Please? I won't get hurt, I promise."

"Don't be silly," snapped Mrs. Leroy. "Burros are rough and dirty and loud. They aren't for ladies!"

Pale but defiant, Fawn stayed aboard Patches, reasoning, "Kathleen's a lady and she rides. Solomon Sal loves burros, too, and ladies don't come any finer than her."

"I only want what's best for you," Fawn's mama contended as the unexpected "lady" compliment echoed through Kathleen's head.

"Then why can't you understand? I want to race. Please, Mama? Please?"

"Down," said her mother.

Shoulders slumping, Fawn dismounted. Kathleen saw the glitter of gathering tears.

"Watch out! Don't walk behind her, she'll kick you!" warned Mrs. Leroy.

Dodging her mother's outstretched hand, Fawn circled behind Patches to dab at her tears. Kathleen caught her breath as Cookie pushed his way through and took Fawn by the hand. He beckoned to Mrs. Leroy. Looking shy but determined, he caught her hand too. Kathleen watched his lips move, but his words were too soft to hear.

Whatever he'd said, he'd startled Mrs. Leroy. Her mouth dropped open, her eyes grew very wide, and she got such a strange look on her face that Kathleen thought for a moment she was either going to start raging again or burst into tears. Finally Mrs. Leroy murmured words even quieter than Cookie's, then she turned and walked away.

Cookie's gaze followed her a moment then came back to Fawn. He lifted her onto Patches's back, put the reins in her hand, and said, "Good luck."

A radiant smile broke through Fawn's tears. She flung her arms around Cookie's neck. "Thanks, Wesley. You're my best friend."

He flushed and patted her knee then moved away. Fawn nodded to the fire chief. "I'm ready."

The chief started moving the barricades out of the way. Kathleen watched in a daze as two boys stretched a ribbon across the road for a starting line. *Kathleen's a lady.*

"Okay, line 'em up!" called the fire chief.

Kathleen's a lady. The words rang over and over in her mind. *A lady. A lady. A lady.* Kathleen looked from the fire chief reaching for the starting gun to Fawn and the little gold pin on her shirt. Her stomach writhed like a pit full of snakes. Ladies didn't spit in the eye of friendship. Ladies didn't sew spiders into their pockets. And ladies didn't make their own luck at the cost of someone else's dignity.

"Wait!" the cry exploded from her lungs. "Hold up just one second!"

Kathleen bailed off Biscuit and left the reins dangling.

111

She raced to the boardwalk in front of the lumber company, took off her vest and carefully tugged the string from her pocket. Gently tucking her vest under the walk where it was dark and secluded, she whispered, "Goodbye, Harriet. Find yourself a new home."

Eighteen

———⬥———

"Okay, kids. This is it. Last call," warned the fire chief.

Biscuit squeezed between two burros and nipped at the starting ribbon. Every bit as eager, Kathleen squinted in the morning sun, visualizing the finish line at the other end of town: a bright smear of paint across the road and another taut ribbon. She strained forward, intent on reaching it first.

The chief raised his arm, the starting gun in hand. "On your marks!"

Kathleen gathered the reins in one sweaty hand. Her free fist clutched the switch. Heart pounding, she locked her knees to Biscuit's fuzzy sides and drew a deep sharp breath.

"Set!"

Her head came down. She reached back with the switch just as the gun popped. Biscuit exploded through the ribbon, flanked by a jenny and a jack. Leaning low, breeze in her hair, Kathleen shouted, "Go Biscuit, go!"

Biscuit stretched out his neck, knowing what she

wanted and eager to deliver. A paper fluttered across the street, startling the jack. He fell back, but Biscuit pounded on. The jenny to their left edged into the lead only to be overtaken by Patches. Third, they were in third!

"Faster!" wailed Kathleen. The earthy scent of burro filled her nostrils as rivals pressed in on both sides. They flew down the street, the cheers of the crowd muted by her thundering heart and eight burros's thundering hooves.

Eyes burning from the dust and the dry wind, Kathleen could feel the heat and the motion and the noise of the pack. Pressing hard. Pressing closer. Gaining, still gaining until they galloped five abreast with Patches narrowly in the lead. "Faster, baby, faster!" pleaded Kathleen, using the switch.

The burro to their left veered off course and faded away. Another stumbled, sending her rider head over heels. Kathleen didn't dare look back. Straining, sides heaving, Biscuit pushed ahead of the pack. He was second only to Patches as they pounded past Cactus Jack's, past the hotel, past the grocery store, and on toward the jail.

"Go, boy, go!" Kathleen raised the switch and let it fall, the finish line almost in sight. Growing nearer! Nearer, as a tiring Biscuit poured out his heart while Patches's lead widened by inches.

"We're almost there, just a little bit more," pleaded Kathleen in despair. "Come on, baby!" She dropped the switch, using only her knees and her hands and her voice.

Each gasp of breath shuddered through Biscuit as he pushed valiantly on. But hopes of victory were dimming, for down that narrow tunnel between Biscuit's ears was a blur of hooves and tail as Patches pounded swiftly toward the finish line. Ten feet. Five. Four. Patches was almost upon the smear of paint when abruptly, she let go a startled bray and skidded to a stop.

Kathleen strained against Biscuit's neck as they flew across the line to victory! Stunned, she wheeled around to see Patches still fighting the painted line, refusing to cross, despite Fawn's urgent pleas. Two, three, four, five burros crossed the finish line and still Patches refused.

Old Coot limped into the street, the first to congratulate her with a thump, thump, thump on the back. "No depth perception, didn't I tell ya? That'll show that durn sidewindin' Slade!"

Chortling, Old Coot stepped out of the way for her family. Mama, Daddy, Gram and Grandpa, and Charlie cheering and hugging and tramping on her toes as they closed in around her. Solomon Sal and Binky joined the happy throng. Still dazed, Kathleen sopped up their pride and affection until her heart was near to bursting. She caught a glimpse of daylight peeking through the bodies encircling her and in it was Captain Slade with a frown as deep as his empty wallet. His friends, winnings in hand, were congratulating one another, for every burro had crossed the line ahead of Patches. The little jenny still stood her ground on the other side. Thinking suddenly of Fawn, Kathleen's pulse skipped as her golden head butted into the family circle.

Startled to see her smiling, Kathleen blurted, "It was the line, wasn't it?"

"She just wouldn't cross," said Fawn regretfully. But she shrugged off the disappointment of losing and

115

smiled. "I got to race, though. And guess what? Wesley asked Mama to marry him!"

"Is *that* what he said to change her mind?" yelped Kathleen.

Fawn nodded. Beaming from ear to ear, she confided, "He said marrying meant sharing decisions, and for his part, he thought I should be allowed to race and that if her fears wouldn't let her enjoy it, she didn't have to stay and watch." Breathless, she added, "Isn't he wonderful?"

Kathleen could see how she'd think that. Especially when measured against the Captain. The Captain! Lest he get away without delivering on his end of the deal, Kathleen left Biscuit in her family's care and rushed to overtake Fawn's uncle.

"About that trailer," she began.

"It'll be in front of your place tomorrow morning," the Captain said curtly.

Kathleen turned away before a grin and an "I told you I'd win," could slip. Being a gracious winner was no less important than being a gracious loser. For a lady, anyway.

Captain Slade made good on his promise, unhitching a trailer on their doorstep right before church the next morning. But oh, what a disappointment! Daddy took one look at the beat-up and broken-down fright on wheels and shook his head.

Mama frowned after the Captain as he drove away. Draping an arm over Kathleen's shoulder, she said, "Darlin', that thing won't make it over the state line let alone across the country."

Daddy ambled over and kicked a tire. It hissed and

116

gave up the ghost. Old Coot, having the reputation of a fair-to-middling eye for such things, ambled up and signed its death warrant, saying, "You'll have to pay to have that dad-blamed piece of junk hauled off."

It was such a letdown after the joy of yesterday, Kathleen sat down on the boardwalk and cried. Old Coot shuffled off, using the Captain's name in vain and muttering dark threats that alarmed Mama so much so that she sent Daddy after him just to be sure the old prospector wouldn't make good on any of them.

Kathleen wiped her eyes on her skirt and wimpered, "It isn't fair."

Mama was looking blue, too. She had been ever since their company'd left yesterday afternoon. Sitting down beside her, she made no reference to Biscuit at all, rather murmured, "Did I ever tell you darlin', about leaving Illinois?"

Kathleen shook her head no, her throat too thick for words.

"Use a tissue." Mama handed her one, snapped her pocketbook closed, and resumed her story. "We had to go because of Grandpa Dave's job building the road. Razz stayed with a family in Shirley. I missed him something awful!"

"Did he miss you, too?" Kathleen asked.

"He never said so, but I guess he did, for one Christmas he wrote and said he was coming to see me. It was Depression time. He didn't have a job or any money. Sophie and Dave doubted he'd come. But I kept praying, believing he'd make it."

"Did he?" asked Kathleen.

Mama smiled. "Oh, he came all right and he caused all sorts of commotion."

"Was it fun?"

"Well, it wasn't exactly the Christmas reunion I'd had in mind. But it was special. And it taught me that sometimes we've got to draw our own hands back and just let the good Lord work."

"How?" asked Kathleen.

"Rose Kathleen, you aren't listening," said Mama. She came to her feet, dusted her skirt and said, "Run on in and wash your face, you're going to be late for Sunday School."

Halfway through church, it came to Kathleen. Wedged between Solomon Sal and Mama, she sat on her hands just to show Him she truly was leaving it up to Him. When the last song was sung, Mama invited Miss Solomon to have lunch with them. Before the meal was served, Old Coot was on their doorstep, too.

"We were just about to eat. Come on in and join us, won't you?" Mama invited.

Old Coot came in, though he claimed he wasn't staying. Turning his hat in his hand, he said, "I been thinking, once I settle in here at Cactus Jack's I won't be needing my sheepherder's wagon. It ain't all that purty to look at, and it'll slow you down some, but it's road worthy." He inclined his head to Kathleen and added, "I'd like the girl here to have it."

Kathleen's joy over the provided transportation for Biscuit faded a bit throughout a week of packing and divvying up stuff they couldn't take, and it just about withered altogether on the morning of their departure. The sheepherder's wagon was hitched to the truck with Biscuit stamping his foot inside.

Old Coot and Cookie shook Daddy's hand. Miss Solomon hugged Mama, and Fawn pressed an envelope

118

into Kathleen's hand, saying, "It's a letter for Charlie and a school picture. You're stopping there, aren't you?"

Kathleen nodded. They were planning to stop for a brief stay first at Gram and Grandpa's in Oklahoma and then again at Charlie's home in Missouri. Daddy said that pulling the sheepherder's wagon was going to slow them down, so they might just as well make the most of the trip by sightseeing and spending some time with family.

Daddy climbed behind the steering wheel and beckoned for Mama and Kathleen to join him. Wanting to sit by the door, Kathleen let Mama in first.

Miss Solomon clasped her hand through the open window as Daddy started the motor. "Lord willing, you'll be back someday. Until then, we'll be looking at the same stars."

"If I can see them through the trees," said Kathleen.

Mama smiled quietly and patted her knee. "You'll like the trees, you'll see."

"Let's write," called Fawn as the truck started to roll.

Mistrusting the sobs gathering in her throat, Kathleen could only nod. Biscuit gave a startled bray as they lurched away from the curb. Eyes burning, Kathleen leaned out the window, drinking in one last look of Cactus Jack's and the friends she loved. Cookie was tying Fawn's shoe. But Old Coot lifted his hand and called, "So long, Desert Rat."

"Desert Rose," said Miss Solomon. She smiled and waved her hat. "Keep blooming, child. Keep on blooming."